Sandra
Waggoner

Sable
CREEK
PRESS

Cover and text design by Diane King, dkingdesigner.com
Cover photo: © Getty Images/iStockphoto

Scripture taken from the King James Version. Public domain.

Published by Sable Creek Press, Glendale, Arizona

sablecreekpress.com

Library of Congress Control Number: 2016961087

ISBN 978-0-9974953-7-9

Printed in the United States of America.

THIS book is dedicated to my mama and daddy who met in Plevna, Kansas when a group of young people were going to have Saturday night fun in Hutchinson, Kansas. The car was packed when they stopped to pick up my mom and her sister, Lillian, and dusk had already settled. Mama opened the back door and unwittingly sat on my dad's lap. They had never met. My dad said, "There is room on the seat." As always, my mom giggled.

Both my mom and dad reside in Heaven now, and they are the reason I will join them one day. They started going to church every time the doors were open the year I was born.

I have a verse that reminds me of my daddy, Arthur Charles Davis:

Ps. 84:10 "For a day in thy courts is better than a thousand. I had rather be a doorkeeper in the house of my God, than to dwell in the tents of wickedness."

My daddy was an usher at church. I guess that is a doorkeeper. I know he valued those doors and the people who walked through them.

I have several verses for my mama, Laura Mae Davis:

Pro. 18:24 "A man that hath friends must shew himself friendly: and there is a friend that sticketh closer than a brother."

My mama picked my husband out before I knew him. I will never know how many meals she cooked for Greg, or how many prayers she prayed just so I would realize he was the one for me. Thank you, Mama, for recognizing the best thing in my life. You were more than a friend who prayed for God's finest for me. You did good 'cause I love him!!!

Pro. 17:22 "A merry heart doeth good like a medicine."

I believe my mama giggles in Heaven today, and maybe it is the sound of the tinkling rain through the leaves of Cottonwood trees.

BOOKS BY SANDRA WAGGONER

DANGER AT WOLF ROCK

SON OF AN HONEST MAN

JOURNEY TO THE FAR ISLANDS

GATLIN FIELDS SERIES:
MAGGIE'S TREASURE
IN THE SHADOW OF THE ENEMY
WHEN SECRETS COME HOME
AFTER THE DUST SETTLES

CALENDAR SERIES:
JULY IS COMING
WINDS OF SEPTEMBER
GIFT OF DECEMBER

Contents

1

The First Day of School

JULY'S tummy tightened, and her skin tingled as she slammed the screen door behind her. She knew that would bring Grams. She ran across the porch and jumped to the gravel drive, twisting the top of her sack lunch, then unrolling it and twisting it again. She was heading to the tree row to hide. No one could make her go to school.

Grams stepped out onto the porch with a kitchen towel in her hand. "July, I know you don't believe me, but you're going to like it. In fact, you're even going to have fun. Levi and Celie do," Grams encouraged.

July turned to look at Grams. "Levi and Celie aren't the new kid in school. They know everyone, and they know all the rules." What July didn't tell Grams was that Levi did not like school, and he had given her plenty of good reasons why. Celie had said it was his own fault; he had spent so much time standing in the corner or getting his fingers rapped by the wooden ruler.

Gramps strode from the barn carrying a shovel. He winked at July as he insisted, "It's going to be a fine day, young lady. You put a smile on that face and say a prayer. Nothing will stand in your way."

July walked to Gramps and begged, "Why can't you and Grams teach me at home? I'm a fast learner."

"July, the teacher will do a better job of it, and there are kids to learn with. You'll like that," Gramps replied.

"Gramps." July spied Levi and Celie cutting across the yard in her direction. She dropped her voice to a whisper so they could not hear. "I'm ten years old, but Levi said I have to learn with the six-year-old squirts because I've only been to school while I was in the orphanage, and that was only for six months. You could just teach me at home this year to catch me up on things, so then I could learn with kids my own age next year."

Gramps's eyebrows rose. "Levi said that, did he?"

"Yes, sir," July answered promptly.

"Levi," Gramps called while clamping his hand on July's shoulder to keep her in place.

Levi stopped in his tracks, a worried look crossing his face.

"Levi, front and center," Gramps ordered.

Slowly Levi walked to stand in front of Gramps. "Yes, sir."

"I want you to tell your cousin exactly who she is going to be studying with," Gramps instructed.

Levi answered, "With all of us, I guess."

"All of us? Does that mean you study with the six-year-old squirts? Are you a part of that group, Levi?" Gramps challenged.

Levi swallowed. "No, sir."

Gramps continued, "Levi, how does it work then?"

Levi glared at July. "Miss Smith puts us in groups. The younger ones are together, then the middle group and then the older ones."

July scowled at her cousin.

Gramps asked, "So, Levi, which group will July be in?"

Levi looked at the ground. "She will be with Celie and me."

Gramps pushed the hat back on his head. "Now, Levi, do I need to walk the three of you to school, or can you get there without any more horror stories to scare your cousin?"

"We can get there, Gramps. No more horror stories," Levi promised as he took out walking way in front of the girls.

Gramps shook his head. "Girls, you had better watch out for that Levi. He is all boy."

"Yes, sir," Celie answered. "Come on, July. I'll let you in on a secret. I think Levi has a crush on Miss Smith. He's always watching her when she isn't looking. He never listens because he is so goo-gle-eyed, and I think that is why he gets into so much trouble. But DO NOT TELL HIM I TOLD YOU."

July shrugged. "I won't tell him." But she knew she wouldn't forget it. That was good information should she need to use it, and if Levi pulled another 'school' trick, it would come in handy.

"Promise? Cross your heart and hope to die?" Celie demanded.

"Celie, I promise," July responded while taking her finger and crossing her heart. There was no way she could sneak into the tree row to ditch school now. Celie would tell.

At the school, July counted nine kids that were about her age. With Celie, Levi and herself there would be twelve. At least it wasn't thirteen. Thirteen was supposed to be unlucky, and she needed all the luck she could get.

The teacher stepped out and rang the bell. "Good morning. I am Miss Smith, and we are going to have a great year together. I would like you to line up in three lines. All of the students who are ages six, seven and eight line up right here," she instructed. She pointed to her left and then continued, "Those who are nine, ten, eleven and twelve line up in the middle. The rest of you line up on my right side." When the lines were quiet, Miss Smith led them into the school and told each group where to sit. She then did a bit of rearranging according to personalities. When she could, she arranged the students by gender: boy, girl, boy, girl.

July found herself sitting by a dark-haired, tall boy in overalls. He was quick to smile, dimples popping on each side of his mouth.

Then he winked at her. July gasped and felt her blood warming her face. The boy laughed, and she turned away just in time to see a girl who had walked in late and stood, somewhat snobbishly, at the empty chair beside July. Thirteen. This late girl made the unlucky number thirteen in their group.

"Priscilla!" She frowned down at July. "I am Priscilla Overton," she hissed. "I saw you flirting with Franklin. I will warn you only this one time. I have dibs on Franklin, so stay away from him."

"What?" July was shocked.

"You heard me. He is the only boy besides Dooby in our group who is taller than I am. So, he is mine. You stay away from him."

"And exactly who are you?" July asked.

Priscilla sighed. "I told you. I am Priscilla Overton, and my father is Jud Overton, the banker. In fact, we own the bank."

Miss Smith rapped on her desk and called, "Prissy, you know the rules. There will be no talking, and no more tardies. This is the first day of school, and you already have a tardy. I don't want it to happen again." Miss Smith shook her head.

Prissy smiled sweetly. "Yes, Miss Smith. I was explaining a few of the rules to our new girl. She asked, and she needed to know them. I didn't want her to get in trouble her first day of school."

July's mouth dropped open.

Miss Smith sighed. "Thank you, Prissy. Now if you will have a seat, we will go over the rules together."

"I did not ask," July muttered under her breath.

"Girls, we do not converse with one another without permission," Miss Smith reminded as she turned to the blackboard.

"We will continue this at recess," Prissy threatened as she gave July a wide, wicked smile.

Before July could retort, Levi thumped her on the back of the head. July turned. Levi mouthed the words, "Leave Prissy alone. She is trouble."

"Levi?" Miss Smith turned from the blackboard. "Surely you have not forgotten all our rules from last year. We are not going to have another 'corner' year, are we?" she asked.

"No, ma'am, Miss Smith," Levi assured her.

The rest of the morning went smoothly with introductions and instructions, but July began to think lunch would never come. Her tummy rumbled, and Prissy smirked beside her. When Miss Smith finally dismissed them, July grabbed her lunch sack and headed outside. She plopped on the grass with Celie and pulled out her biscuit with bacon sandwich. A shadow fell across her face, and she looked up. The tall, dark-haired boy stood above her. He had Levi with him. "Levi, introduce me to your cousin," he said.

"What?" Levi was appalled. "She's a girl, Franklin."

The boy's dimples rippled as he acknowledged, "I know."

July groaned.

Levi shrugged. "This is my cousin, June July Calendar. July, this is …" Levi swallowed. "This WAS my friend, Franklin D. Franklin."

Franklin stretched out his hand. "Shake? That's what friends do."

July didn't really want to shake his hand, but she didn't know what else to do. Slowly she stood, spit in her hand and stuck it out to Franklin.

"All right. A real hand shake," he said as he winked, grabbed July's hand and shook.

Prissy marched up to July. "I warned you, July. I will send you clear back to January!" With those words, she wadded up her fist and belted July in the eye. July tumbled over and sprawled in the grass, but not for long. She bounced to her feet and charged Prissy and punched her in the stomach. Together they rolled until Miss Smith ran down the porch steps, across the grass and grabbed an ear of each of the girls.

"That is enough! Girls do not solve problems by fighting. It is very unladylike conduct. Both of you march into the school right now and write a note to your parents. And it will be a sign and return note," Miss Smith warned.

"But it was not my fault, Miss Smith. July attacked me," Prissy pleaded.

July gasped. With her hands on her hips she bellowed, "You hit me first, and I didn't do a thing to you."

Prissy stepped nose to nose with July and whispered menacingly, "I warned you. Keep your grubby hands off of Franklin. He is mine!" she demanded. "July, I saved your life. I was trying to shoo the biggest bumble bee away from you. He was about to land on your forehead."

"There was no bumble bee, and no one shoos away anything with a fist," July growled.

"There was too a bumble bee, wasn't there, Franklin?" Prissy asked innocently, turning to the tall boy.

"Bumble bee?" Franklin shrugged. "All I saw was gobs of dark hair and freckles. Now that's a girl who knows how to shake a hand and have it stick. Wow. Oh, wow!" Franklin whistled.

Prissy turned purple, yelled and charged Franklin, but Franklin sidestepped. Prissy ran instead into Levi, who toppled to the ground and scooted on his behind for at least three feet.

"Prissy!" Miss Smith yelled. "Get into the school now and start writing."

The whole schoolyard was stunned into silence. With an arrogant flare, Prissy tossed her bobbed, blonde hair. Then she turned, glided across the yard, up the steps and into the school. Everyone watched her go then turned to stare at July.

Miss Smith blew the bangs of her hair and looked toward heaven. "Lord, this is only the first day of school. You are going to have to help me."

Prissy stood in the doorway. "Miss Smith, doesn't July have to come and write, too? That is not fair to me if she doesn't have to, and my father won't like that. He's on the school board, you know."

"Worry about yourself, Prissy. I will take care of July," Miss Smith responded calmly. She held her hand out to the new girl. "Come with me. It seems you need a cool cloth for that eye."

Absently, July patted her mother's ring dangling on a chain beneath her dress. She gazed at her teacher and insisted, "There wasn't a bee, Miss Smith."

Miss Smith sighed. "Bee or not, you are going to have a pretty healthy shiner there."

July tried again. "Miss Smith, Prissy slugged me for no reason, and if someone slugs me, I'm going to fight."

"July, has your grandfather taught you about turning the other cheek?" Miss Smith asked as she studied July's face.

July shook her head. "I guess not yet."

Miss Smith nodded her head. "I am thinking he will when he reads that sign and return note of yours."

July's heart dropped. She knew she would be in trouble. She had to figure a way to word the note so Gramps would know it was not her fault. It was self-defense. If only she could have hidden in the tree row the way she had planned.

"And I will read the note before you leave school today," Miss Smith informed July. Together they walked into the school.

Franklin watched them disappear. Slowly he whistled. "Levi, you are so lucky. Your cousin is beautiful."

Levi scrunched his face in wonder. "July? Beautiful? She's a girl."

"She sure is." Franklin almost drooled.

"She will get you in so much trouble it's not funny," Levi warned. "She gets me into trouble all the time."

"Trouble like that? Bring it on," Franklin responded as he shoved his hands in his overall pockets and headed for the school.

Levi stood and shook his head. "Who would have figured that? What happened to Franklin over the summer?" he wondered.

The Sign and Return Note

"**JULY**, you are in so much trouble," Celie said as she grabbed July's arm the minute they stepped off the porch of the school. July wadded up the note and threw it in the shrubs.

"You can't throw that note away, July. It has to be signed by either Gramps or Grams, and maybe even both. Miss Smith will ask for it first thing in the morning," said Celie.

"I don't care. I don't plan to go to school in the morning," July said.

"You can't skip school. Besides, this is a little town. Everybody knows what goes on here. Gramps might already know," said Celie.

July stopped and poked her finger at Celie. "If you tell on me, I'll tell everybody Levi has a crush on Miss Smith, and then Levi will know you told me."

Celie was stunned. "You can't do that. You promised, and you crossed your heart, and you hoped to die," Celie reminded July.

"I'd rather die than go back to school with that Prissy," July said.

"It'll be better tomorrow. Look, you were worried no one would notice you or want to know you." Celie continued, "Everyone knows you, and I think Franklin really likes you."

July stopped and turned toward Celie. Her hands were in fists on her hips as she leaned in closer to her cousin. "Sure. Everybody knows me. I'm the girl with the black eye," July retorted.

Celie straightened her shoulders. "Yes, you are, and everybody admires you. You stood up to Prissy. I don't think anyone has ever done that before. July, you are a kind of hero to the rest of us," said Celie.

"Hero?" July pursed her lips together. "It must not take much to be a hero in this town."

"Well, that is exactly what you are," Celie said cheerfully.

July turned and started walking. Celie studied July before she asked, "What are you going to tell Gramps and Grams about your shiner?"

"I don't know," said July. "Maybe I ran into the slippery slide at lunch break, or I tripped and fell off the steps. I'll make up something." July slowed as she realized that making up something would be a lie. Lies didn't go over very well with Grams and Gramps, and the lies made her feel funny inside.

Celie stopped this time and grabbed July's arm. "You had better think about this. You are already in trouble with the sign and return note, but when Gramps finds out you're telling lies to stay out of trouble … well, I wouldn't want to be in your shoes," Celie said.

"But the fight was not my fault. Why should I get in trouble?" July complained.

"Explain it to Grams and Gramps. They love you, and they are pretty fair. You might be surprised at what will happen if you trust them," Celie offered.

"Do you really think so?" July asked.

Celie nodded.

A gust of wind whipped their skirts, and both girls looked to the skies. From the south, a dark cloud clung to the horizon. Celie groaned. "Not again, not another dust storm. We'll be eating Oklahoma dirt for supper. We'd better get home quick."

July paused. "First, I'm going back to get that note. I'll try trusting Grams and Gramps like you said."

Celie smiled. The wind blew her hair across her face, and she tugged a strand from her mouth. "I'm coming with you, but we'd better run," Celie urged.

The wind swept through the dry grass of the playground. Swings swung with ghostly riders, and the merry-go-round turned on its own accord. Miss Smith closed the door and hurriedly crossed the school porch and ran down the steps.

"Wait," July whispered as she grabbed Celie's arm. "I don't want Miss Smith to see me." The girls plastered themselves against the side of the outhouse and watched as a young man rounded the corner of the school.

"Hello, Miss Smith. I'm a bit tardy for school, but I'm not too late to walk you home, am I?" the gentleman asked. Miss Smith smiled and laughed.

The gentleman reached out, took her hand and pressed it to his lips. "Amanda, you look beautiful. How was your first day back at school?"

Miss Smith shook her head. "My first day? Would you believe I had to break up a fight at lunch, and it was between two girls? Of course, one of those girls was Priscilla Overton. I've never seen her fight before, but that is only because no one would fight her."

The gentleman chuckled. "So, now Miss Priscilla has someone who's not afraid of her?"

Miss Smith nodded. "Yes, she does. July Calendar, and I believe she has led a very rough life, so she's got a lot of spunk. I think she is honest, and I like her. She is the orphan taken in by her grandparents, Ezra and May Calendar."

16

"Ahh, the Pastor. If anyone can handle an orphan, the Calendars can do it."

A burst of wind claimed Miss Smith's skirt and tangled it about her ankles. Swiftly, the young man caught her before she tripped and fell. "We had better get you home," he said as he scanned the skies. "I wish it were rain coming, but it has the smell of dust."

The girls waited until they were out of sight. Celie spoke first. "Wow. I didn't know Miss Smith had a beau. I don't think anyone else knows either."

"It isn't any of your business, so you best not tell everyone." July suddenly felt like protecting Miss Smith. What she had said about July being honest tugged at her heart.

Celie smiled. "You heard her say she liked you. I told you Miss Smith was nice. I think she'll stand up for you." Then Celie pleaded, "Please come back to school. You can ask Miss Smith for a seat away from ol' Prissy, and I think she'll give it to you."

July shrugged. "Maybe, but right now I have to find that sign and return note."

The skies were getting blacker, and the wind was howling as the girls returned to the school. Talking only allowed mud to gather in the mouth. July felt the grit, yet she still loved the way it tasted of rain. They searched the bushes but found no note.

"We've got to get home while we still can. The storm is coming on strong," Celie yelled.

"One more time through the bushes," pleaded July. "I know I tossed it down somewhere around here."

"Hurry, July!" Celie begged.

"You can go on without me. I'll be fine," July shouted.

"No. We have to go home together to make sure we get home." Celie looked as if she were ready to cry.

July gave in. "If we must, but no note means for sure I can't come back to school tomorrow."

"We'll work it out, July," Celie promised.

There was no more talking. They battled against the wind, the dirt, and the flying debris the whole way home. At the tree row which separated their houses, they parted. July watched Celie climb the porch steps before she turned and ran to her own back porch.

Grams swung the door open, and July rushed inside. The wind held the heavy door in its grip until July helped Grams pull the door closed from inside. One glance at Grams's face told July she was worried. "Child, where have you been?" Grams asked. "You should have been home long before now."

"I left something at school, so Celie and I went back to get it. Then we couldn't find it, and the storm was rolling in. We had to fight the wind to get here. I watched Celie get to their porch before I came in," July blurted without taking a breath. She had told the truth, even though she left out some of the important parts. She lowered her head and kept her hair over her black eye.

"Good. Celie made it home, too. Sybil sent Levi over looking for his sister about thirty minutes ago. I am glad both of you are safe, so I won't have to worry anymore," Grams responded as she wrapped her arms about July. July was glad she had told the truth.

"How was your first day of school?" Grams asked.

This was the moment July had been dreading. Her heart began a dull thudding which seemed to echo all through her body. She wanted to tell the whole truth, but all she seemed to be able to do was mutter something about school being "fine."

The door burst open, and July nearly jumped out of her skin. Gramps strode in and slammed the door against the wind. He smiled at Grams and then turned to July. "How was school today?" he asked.

July could feel deep in her bones that Gramps must know. She kept her head lowered as she wondered who could have ratted on her. Would Levi have swung by the church and told Gramps? She didn't think Miss Smith and her beau would have stopped by because they were trying to beat the storm. Celie was with July, so it wasn't Celie.

"Well?" Gramps walked over to the table where July sat.

July dropped her gaze to the table top. "I guess it was all right."

"All right?" Gramps pulled out a chair for Grams, then he sat himself. "Why don't you tell us about this 'all right' day?"

"I didn't have to sit with the six-year-old squirts," July offered.

"Good," Gramps replied.

"There are thirteen in our group," July continued.

Gramps raised his eyebrows. "Lucky thirteen, is it?"

July licked her lips. "Thirteen isn't so lucky."

"And?" Gramps prodded.

"It was a normal school day, nothing special," July let the words tumble.

"Nothing special?" asked Gramps. "Anything else happen?"

July shook her head.

Gramps leaned back in his chair and drummed his fingers against the kitchen table, waiting. From inside his overalls pocket he pulled a wadded piece of paper and tossed it to the middle of the table. Everyone's attention was drawn to the paper while silence as thick as the dirt storm outside settled over the room. July felt the fire from the kitchen stove on her back. She heard the wind raging outside, but it was nothing compared to the raging inside her body.

3

The Bible Lesson

GRAMPS watched as July looked up from the wadded paper. The girl was speechless. "Does this belong to you?" Gramps asked.

July looked up at him from behind her hair, remembering her promise. With a silent prayer, she began, "Yes, sir." Then with wonder she asked, "How did you get that?"

"I am the one asking the questions, young lady, and I want to know why someone else brought this to me instead of you, and why is it all wadded up?" Gramps questioned.

July pressed her lips together. This truth thing was not so easy, but she had told Celie she was going to do it. "I wadded it up, and I threw it on the ground. But Celie had a talk with me and told me I should tell the truth 'cause you and Grams love me and would believe me."

"Yet you threw it away, and I suspect it was so we wouldn't know about it. July, not telling is as bad as deciding to tell a lie." Gramps shook his head in disappointment.

"Celie and I went back to look for it, but we couldn't find it. That's why I got home late." July turned to her grandmother. "Right, Grams, I got home right before Gramps came in the door."

Grams looked at Gramps and nodded in agreement.

"And you were going to tell us what this note says?" Gramps asked.

"Yes, sir," July insisted.

Gramps reached to the middle of the table and pulled the note to himself. He unwadded the tight ball of paper and ironed it out with his hand. Slowly he began to read:

Dear Grams and Gramps,

 I got in trouble today at school for belting Priscilla Overton. She deserved it. She hit me first, so I slugged her. Miss Smith said I had to write you a sign and return note. Would you please sign this note because I have to return it?

   Sincerely,

   June July Calendar

P.S. She said I had to say I was sorry.

The End.

For the first time, July looked at Grams and tucked her hair fully behind her ears. Grams sucked in her breath. "July, that is not dust on your face, is it? You have a black eye!"

"Yes, ma'am, but I'm betting Prissy has a black belly," July hesitantly added, pressing her lips together.

Grams didn't crack a smile. "July, young ladies do not settle their differences by slugging, belting or punching."

"But she hit me first. What am I supposed to do, say 'thank you for this black eye, and can we talk now?'" July asked in frustration.

Gramps, with a spark of fire in his eyes, took over the conversation. "Young lady, you will not speak like that to your grandmother. You will apologize, and you will listen very carefully. Your grandmother loves you, and she is trying to teach you a lesson about how young ladies respond in difficult situations. Do you understand?"

July nodded. "I'm sorry, Grams, but I still don't understand what I'm supposed to do. I think Prissy would have killed me if I let her." July continued helplessly, "When we lived in the old buildings and the alleys in Kansas City, I learned to stand up for Mama and myself because there wasn't anybody else who would. 'Polite' was something we couldn't always afford. Mama told me to do what I had to do."

Tears were trickling down Grams's cheeks, and Gramps had to clear his throat before he could answer. "July, you don't live in the alleys anymore. I know you did what you had to do in Kansas City, but things are different here in Plevna. We let the authority take care of disputes."

"The police? They weren't at school," July said.

Gramps smiled. "And I hope they never have to be at school. I was referring to your teacher, Miss Smith. She is your authority at school."

"But, Gramps, she wasn't out on the playground when Prissy jumped me," July explained.

"She wasn't?" Gramps asked.

"No. She told us all to grab our lunches, head out to the play-ground, and she would follow in a minute. Levi had just introduced me to his friend, Franklin, and we were shaking hands. That's when Prissy slugged me. I didn't even know she was going to do it. I sure didn't start the fight. You can ask Levi and Celie. They will tell you," July explained.

Gramps leaned back in his chair and hooked his thumbs through the straps of his overalls. He seemed to be thinking things over. Finally, he leaned forward with his elbows on the table and stroked his chin. "July, I believe you about not starting the fight, but what I want to know now is, why this?" Gramps turned the note toward July and pointed to the bottom of the paper.

July gasped. There was a picture drawn of an ugly, bug-eyed woman with frayed hair and spots on her face. Her teeth were close to fangs, and dribble oozed from the side of her mouth. Underneath the picture was written: **Miss Smith**. An arrow was penciled in pointing to the picture with the words: **I hate Miss Smith**!!!

"I did not draw that picture, and I did not write that. Honest, Gramps. You have to know I didn't draw this," July was begging him to believe her.

"Then who would? It is your note. The handwriting is like yours. It was wadded up and thrown down. Who else would do it?" Gramps asked.

"I don't know." July shook her head in confusion.

"Ezra, who brought the note to the church?" Grams asked. "Maybe that person would have a clue."

Gramps nodded. "Maybe, May. The girl didn't give me her name, and I don't recall her coming to church services. Yet, she might have. Kids grow and change. Let's see." Gramps crinkled his face as he tried to remember. "She was taller than July, I think, and she had short, blonde hair, almost tow-headed."

July gasped. "That description fits Priscilla Overton. She's the one who slugged me!"

"Priscilla Overton?" Grams and Gramps asked together.

"Yes, and I bet she's the one who drew that picture! Wait until I get ahold of her!" July jumped up and began pacing.

"Whoa, young lady. You are not going to 'get ahold' of that girl," Gramps stated firmly.

"But look what Prissy has done. She put me right in a fix to get in trouble," July insisted angrily.

"July, you are not in trouble," Grams and Gramps agreed.

Wildly July still paced. "Well, not with you, but it is a sign and return note. Miss Smith may agree with you about who drew that picture. I want to beat Prissy up and teach her a lesson."

"I think you are the one who needs a lesson, July. We don't search out people to beat up," Gramps said.

"She hit me first," July growled.

Gramps shook his head. "It doesn't matter. God doesn't want you to seek Prissy out and beat her up. He teaches us to turn the other cheek," Gramps said.

July stopped and stared at Gramps. "That's like what Miss Smith said. She asked me if you had taught me to turn the other cheek."

"Come have a seat," Gramps said as he patted a chair. "Grams, bring us the Good Book."

Grams smiled and winked at July. "I wondered how long it would be before Gramps let you have that lesson. It's been a coming."

It didn't take Gramps long before he was thumbing through the pages of his Bible. He knew exactly where he was going. "Now, July, I could probably quote this to you, but I think it will mean more if you know it was God who said it and not me. Right here in Matthew 5:38." Gramps pointed at the place. "I want you to read this loud and clear."

July began, "Ye have heard that it hath been said, An eye for an eye, and a tooth for a tooth: But I say unto you, That ye resist not evil: but whosoever shall smite thee on thy right cheek, turn to him the other also."

Gramps studied July. "Do you understand what the scripture is saying?" Gramps hesitated and then answered the question before July got a chance. "It means if someone like Prissy gives you a black eye, you are to turn the other cheek."

July was aghast. "You mean I'm supposed to let her hit the other side of my face?"

Gramps nodded.

"Who wrote this anyway?" July demanded.

Gramps smiled. "Matthew wrote it, but Jesus said it."

July mumbled, "He sure didn't live in Kansas City."

"No, July, he did not, but he died a horrible death on the cross, and he did it without saying a word in his defense. What he did say, after the mob had laughed at him, yanked his beard from his face, whipped him horribly, slapped him, spit upon him and nailed him to the cross, was, 'Father, forgive them.' July, Jesus is our example. If Jesus could do it, we can do it, too."

July was shaking her head. "But, Prissy? You don't know Prissy."

Gramps moved his finger further down the page. "Read this, July."

July found where Gramps had landed his finger and began reading, "Ye have heard that it hath been said, Thou shalt love thy neighbor, and hate thine enemy. But I say unto you, Love your enemies, bless them that curse you, do good to them that hate you, and pray for them which despitefully use you, and persecute you; That ye may be the children of your father which is in heaven: for he maketh the sun to rise on the evil and the good, and sendeth rain on the just and the unjust."

July felt a sick lump in her tummy. She wondered, *Is this how I'm supposed to treat Prissy?* Even if she decided to do this thing called 'turn the other cheek,' Prissy was not going to make it easy. July figured she was going to have to get used to black eyes and bloody noses. At least she didn't have to turn the other nose. July felt a tiny smile tug at her lips, but she hid it from Grams and Gramps. She didn't think they would see anything funny about this.

July let everything soak in before she asked, "So, if you won't teach me at home, and I have to go to school, I think I'm going to be needing a bunch of cool rags and bandages."

Grams smiled. "July, I think you had best stay close to Levi and Celie. Then if you can't get to Miss Smith, have one of them run for her."

Gramps added, "July, your best weapon can be prayer. Right now you think your punches can save you, but the punches our Heavenly Father gives can pack a wallop."

"God punches?" July whistled. "Boy, I am learning more about God every day."

Gramps laughed. "Yes, he does. If you will let Him, God will fight your battles for you. You will be wishing you would have had God on your side in Kansas City."

When the laughter settled, July asked, "Gramps, why didn't Mama know about God fighting your battles for you?"

Grams rubbed her forehead. Gramps sobered. "Honey, your mama knew. At least she knew it up here." Gramps pointed to his head. "When you start to practice what God tells you to do, then you cement it in here." Gramps thumped the place in his chest which covered his heart. "Once you cement God's words in your heart by doing what He has told you to do, you have a foundation on which to build your faith and make it stronger. Too many people know it in their head, but they never put it to work in their hearts. The only way to prove God's Word is true is to do what He tells you to do. July, do you understand that?"

"I think so, Gramps. It's like 'practice what you preach' only it's 'practice what God preaches.'"

Gramps nodded his head in agreement. "Out of the mouths of babes. That will preach, July. That will preach."

The storm outside the walls of their home had tuckered out right about the time the storm around their kitchen table sighed and settled. Home was a nice place to be.

4

The Vocabulary Lesson

I**T** was agreed that Gramps would walk to school early with July and converse with Miss Smith. Powdered silt had settled on the grass, and it exploded with each footstep. The sun filtered through a thin film of dust hovering in the sky, muting the colors of early morning. The birds had not given up on the day. They chirped, and July thought they must be praising the Lord. That gave her hope. With God and Gramps, Miss Smith would have to believe her. What a team: God and Gramps. July slipped a peek at her grandfather. His lips were firm as he stared straight ahead. She decided he must be thinking about the meeting with Miss Smith. Was he troubled? July watched him a little longer before she asked, "Gramps, are you worried about this meeting?"

"Worried? I don't think so, July, but it never hurts to go over things with the Lord. I sure want Him to be a part of our meeting, too. I guess you could say I was inviting Him to join us," Gramps said.

July laughed. "You know, Gramps, some people would think you are touched in the head because you're always talking to someone you can't see and no one else can see either."

"Oh, but I see what He does. He answers my prayers all the time so that I know He's right here with me. I can almost see Him," Gramps replied.

July twisted her head to study Gramps. "See Him?"

Gramps nodded. "There is a scripture that goes like this: 'He that hath my commandments, and keepeth them, he it is that loveth me: and he that loveth me shall be loved of my Father, and I will love him, and I will manifest myself to him.'"

"Manifest? What is manifest? Is it like a ghost or something?" July asked.

Gramps chuckled. "I had to look up that word myself. I liked the definition so well I chose to memorize it. It means 'readily perceived by the senses and especially by the sense of sight, or easily understood or recognized by the mind.' July, the closer you get to God, the more you will know he lives and walks with you."

"Manifest." July repeated the word, letting it soak into her mind.

Gramps slowed. "Seems your friend beat us here."

July looked ahead. Skipping down the steps of the school was Prissy. "She is not my friend. Enemy is a better word," July said as she tightened her fists.

Quietly, so only July could hear, Gramps said, "Friend or foe, it doesn't matter with God. He expects you to turn the other cheek."

The lady backing out of the schoolhouse door was clearly Prissy's mother. "Miss Smith, I consider it your duty to put that little piece of alley trash as far away from my daughter as possible. It is clear she incites disruption, and I'll not have Priscilla be a part of it," said the woman.

Gramps stopped. With a look of warning for July, he asked, "Might we have a word with you, Miss Smith?"

The woman turned around and let her glare travel from the top of July to the bottom before she stepped out of the doorway so Gramps could get inside.

"Surely, Pastor Calendar." Miss Smith smiled and turned back to Prissy's mother. "Thank you for your concern. I will see the matter is taken care of."

"Of course you will." Mrs. Overton smiled. As she passed Gramps, she spoke lowly, "A pastor should be a better keeper of his family flock, Mr. Calendar."

Gramps cleared his throat. "Thank you for those words of wisdom, Mrs. Overton."

As she brushed by and down the steps, Gramps winked at July and touched his cheek. July laughed. Prissy made sure no one was watching before she walked to July and whispered, "Aren't you glad I found your note for you?"

July wanted to punch her. Instead, she slowly relaxed her fists; forgetting she held her sack lunch, it dropped to the ground. Like a vulture sweeping down on dead prey, Prissy stomped on the sack, smashing July's lunch. "Oops, I'm so sorry, August or September or whoever you are," Prissy snickered.

July kept her hands clutching her skirt. If Gramps could do it, she could do it. "Thank you." It was hard to not slug Prissy, but it was even harder to control her tongue. "I guess I'll see you when class starts, Sissy ... I mean Kissy."

"You just wait!" Prissy glared.

"Priscilla," Mrs. Overton said. "Get away from that girl and come along or you will be late for school, unless you want to wait here, and I'll bring your lunch to you. But if you wait, go and wait with Miss Smith. You will be safer there."

"I'll come, Mother. I was just telling October how sorry I was that we got off to a bad start." Then she whispered to July, "I will be back."

July stared after Prissy. Lies seemed to tumble out of her mouth with no regrets. It used to be like that for July, but since she knew Jesus, she had found that when she even thought about telling a lie, something inside of her rebelled. Gramps and Grams would say it was the Holy Spirit trying to lead her in the paths of righteousness. As if a light came on, July whispered to herself, "I understand. That must be manifest in action."

Gramps might as well have been whistling when he strode out the door and almost bounced down the steps, if a grandpa could still bounce. He crossed to his granddaughter. "All taken care of. Miss Smith will be watching out for you, which also means she will see anything you do. So you had best put a hold on that temper you seem to be guided by."

July smiled. "Yes, sir." She reached down to pick up her smashed lunch.

"You been playing leap frog with your lunch and miss?" Gramps asked.

"Sure," July answered sarcastically.

"What really happened?" Gramps asked.

"Prissy is what happened. I dropped it on accident, and she whipped right in there and stomped it flatter than a pancake."

Gramps shook his head. "You sure have your work cut out for you. Let me have the sack, and I'll bring you another lunch. Biscuits and bacon is it?"

"It was. It's probably bacon and crumbs now." July laughed.

"Probably so," said Gramps. "I'll eat it with a spoon at home when Grams and I have lunch. No need in wasting good food."

Before Gramps left, he knelt in front of July. "You remember our new rule, 'turn the other cheek,' and our new word, 'manifest.' They will help you through this school day and the rest of your life." Gramps smiled as he kissed her on the cheek.

July watched him walk down the block and turn out of sight. Slowly she went into the school. Miss Smith was writing on the chalkboard, but when she heard July slip in, she turned. "July, let's find you a different seat. If you promise me you will not talk to Celie during classes, I will set you beside her. She is a good student, and I think she will help you with the rules."

"Yes, ma'am. I surely would like that better." July sighed with relief.

Miss Smith pulled a chair to her desk and motioned for July to come and join her. "July, I know Prissy can be difficult. Her mother and father dote on her. I suppose it is because she is their only child. She is barely nine, which makes her at least a year younger than you and maybe more. She is tall for her age, and she hates it. So, please don't make fun of her height anymore."

July was confused. "Miss Smith, I have never made fun of her being tall. A person can't help how tall they are."

"Did you say anything yesterday about her being tall? Did you call her a 'gawky giraffe'?" Miss Smith asked.

"No ma'am. I didn't even know she was going to punch me until she did it. I was shocked to death, and so I slugged her in self-defense," July insisted.

Miss Smith turned her head to one side in thought. "Yesterday, before lunch, I told you two to stop talking. Were you saying anything about a giraffe then?"

"Miss Smith, I didn't even know her. When she stepped in the door, she had it out for me," July explained. "She told me Franklin belonged to her and to keep my grubby paws off of him. Miss Smith, I don't want Franklin. He's a boy."

Miss Smith's mouth twitched. July could tell she wanted to laugh. "July, I understand. I think our best plan is to keep you as far away from Prissy as possible, and maybe as far away from Franklin as possible, too."

"That's fine, Miss Smith." July stood and stretched out her hand. This time she didn't spit to seal the shake because Grams had told her young ladies don't shake with spit, especially another lady's hand.

Celie popped her head through the door. "Hey, July, Gramps had me bring your sack lunch. I guess you forgot it."

July giggled. "I guess you could say that. Thanks, Celie."

"Come on." Celie motioned outside. "Miss Smith hasn't rung the bell yet. Let's go play." Celie headed for the door, and July followed.

"I got to tell you something. Come quick," Celie urged. She ran around the corner and smashed into the middle of Prissy. She bounced off of the taller girl and sprawled in the dirt.

"Watch where you're going, Roof Top," Prissy growled.

Without thinking, July stepped between Celie and Prissy, the Bully. "You watch where you're going, Kissy."

Prissy gasped. Celie gasped, but it was Levi who yelled, "July, NO!"

July came to her senses. She couldn't be caught fighting with Prissy again. Grams and Gramps wouldn't believe she had tried to turn the other cheek. July yanked around, grabbed Celie and ran. Prissy was shouting threats. "You just wait, November!" Then Prissy threw the only thing in her hand. It was her lunch.

With a thud, Prissy's lunch hammered July in the back as she ran. July tripped and tumbled to the ground with Celie landing on top of her. Celie groaned and rolled to the side. "Oh no," she whined as she sat with her legs tangled and her skirt clinging to her knees. She held her hands to the side with juice dripping from them. A chunk of cornbread slid from her hair and plopped down her chin. Prissy's lunch had burst open, and black-eyed peas blended with the dainty pink rose buds of Celie's dress and splashed down her front. In places, there were clumps of mashed cornbread. "Mama is not going to like this," Celie complained.

July felt the warm juice soak into her back. She crawled to her hands and knees. Then she saw Celie and gasped. "I was trying to save you. I'm sorry."

"You may have saved me from Prissy, but now you're going to have to save me from Mama," Celie sobbed.

The other kids had gathered in a circle around the two on the ground.

"Someone had better get Miss Smith," one student suggested.

"I will," a little girl chimed in.

A boy whistled. "Another fight, and it's only the second day of school!"

"Wow, this is going to be a great year," one of the other boys added.

They were an excited crew until Franklin stepped into the circle, followed by his dog. The hunting hound struck a pose pointing right at Celie. Franklin said, "It's just Celie, Moose. Let her be."

But Moose didn't let her be. He wagged his tail, scrambled to Celie and began lapping Prissy's lunch from her face. Celie groaned and tried to get out of the way, but before long they were rolling in the dry grass, and everyone was laughing.

Miss Smith shoved through the line of kids to the middle of the circle. "What happened?" she demanded.

Prissy stood to her feet. "July stole my lunch."

5

The Eavesdropper

AT Prissy's accusation, Miss Smith raised her eyebrows in question. "July?"

July's heart thudded. The only things she could think of to say would not be called "turning the other cheek," but she did remember what Gramps had said about Jesus on the cross. Jesus didn't say anything except, "Father, forgive them."

July looked Prissy square in the eye. "Prissy, I forgive you."

"What?" Prissy steamed, stormed and stomped. "I … I … I wish I had another lunch to throw at you, and this time I would throw it in your face instead of on your back!"

"Prissy? You threw your lunch at the girls?" Miss Smith swallowed a smile. "Thank you for telling me what happened. I guess that will mean another sign and return note for you to take home at the end of the day—after you clean the chalkboard and erasers."

Prissy's mouth dropped open. Then she took a deep breath and closed it. As she turned, her eyes were like lightning as they flashed toward July. "This is not over by a long shot!" she warned.

"Prissy, march into the classroom," Miss Smith ordered.

Prissy marched. July breathed a sigh of relief. Celie was stunned with unbelief. Moose barked and wagged his tail. The rest of the class laughed.

Miss Smith shook her head. "July and Celie, I think it would be best if you both went home and changed," she suggested.

Franklin heehawed. "Why change? Moose already cleaned most of Celie, and it won't take him long to touch up July."

Celie was the first to express her opinion. "Ugh! I'd rather go home and change than have that mangy dog lick me again."

Franklin covered Moose's ears. "Sorry, Moose. Celie is a bit persnickety. I'll bet July wouldn't care, though, would you, July?"

July shrugged. "I've been licked by lots of dogs. I've even fought dogs for food a couple of times."

Franklin studied July's face before he asked, "You fought dogs for food?"

July put her hands on her hips. "And I won. I got the food; they didn't," she boasted.

Franklin whistled. "What a woman."

"Class." Miss Smith clapped her hands to distract the students from July's statement about fighting dogs for food and Franklin's wonder of July. "Let's head inside. July and Celie, we will see you in a little while. If your parents or grandparents need to know more about what happened, I would be glad to talk to them," Miss Smith said.

July stretched her hand out to help Celie to her feet. "I guess we had best get this over with."

Celie tried to brush her dress off. "Mama is going to be very unhappy. I wish I could go to Grams like you do."

July giggled. "Grams is pretty easy on me, but Gramps takes out the Good Book and preaches to me."

"Did you get a lesson last night?" Celie asked.

"What do you think?" July responded.

"On turning the other cheek?" Celie grinned.

"Yep, but it worked. Look who got in trouble: Prissy. I didn't get in trouble this time—other than getting soaked with black-eyed peas." July felt like skipping.

"You're right, and can you believe it? Prissy got so mad she confessed," Celie added gleefully. "Oh, and I remember what I wanted to tell you. Miss Smith's beau's name is Herbert Harms. He's from Hudson, and his family has a farm, and they run a furniture store."

"Celie, how did you find that out?" July asked.

"Sometimes I pretend I'm asleep and listen to what Mama and Daddy talk about. Because of the storm last night, I slept on a palette in their room, only I wasn't asleep while they were talking. It was really easy to listen," Celie said.

"You had better watch out. You'll get in a load of trouble," July cautioned.

"I know, but listen to this: Mama says Miss Smith and Mr. Harms are going to get married. Isn't that romantic?" Celie was beaming with the news.

"I guess it's romantic, but if Miss Smith is married, can she still be our teacher?" July asked.

Celie shrugged. "I don't know, but they won't get married until school is out anyway. We won't have to worry about that."

"What if they move to Hudson?" July shuddered. "Oh, I hope not. Miss Smith is fair, and I trust her." July kicked at the sidewalk.

Celie stopped at the tree row. "Wait for me, and I'll tell Mama I have to hurry because you are waiting. Better yet, come inside with me. Then Mama won't be as likely to scold me," Celie pleaded.

"No," July answered. "Your mama scares me, and she would scold me, too. I'll meet you back out here as fast as I can." July ran to the porch, jumped the few steps, and flew through the door hollering for Grams as she went. A quick search through the house told her Grams was not there, so she would explain things later when she got home from school.

July yanked off her black-eyed pea dress and tossed it in a pile on the floor. From her closet she pulled out the dress she had worn yesterday and slipped it over her head. She only had two school dresses, a Sunday special dress, and a couple of everyday dresses. All but the Sunday dress were made from old flower sacks. Her Sunday dress was special. Grams had brought it out of storage. It was one that had belonged to her mama years ago. Grams had crocheted a cream-colored collar and sewed it to the dress, then she had crocheted matching lace on the edge of the sleeves. With a soft touch, July held the material to her cheek and patted Mama's ring nestled close to her heart beneath her clothing. "I love you, Mama, and I miss you," she whispered before she let the cloth drop.

July ran down the steps and out the door. Things must not have gone well with Celie because she was nowhere in sight. July dropped to Celie's porch steps and waited and waited.

"Finally." July stood when Celie did pop out of the door. "We had better hurry. Miss Smith will wonder if we're coming back at all. Did you get in a bunch of trouble?" July asked.

A smile flickered across Celie's face. "Nope."

"You didn't?"

"Nope. Grams was there, and Mrs. Hastings. They were too busy talking to even notice me." Celie beamed.

"Then what took you so long?" July asked.

"I was listening." Celie was proud of herself.

"You'll get yourself into a mess if you don't stop eavesdropping," July warned.

"Oh, but you gotta hear what they were talking about. Mrs. Hastings and her husband own the five-and-dime store, but in the back they have jewelry—real jewelry, not the fake stuff. Guess who bought a ring?" Celie was glowing.

July shrugged. "Celie, how would I know?"

Celie threw her hands over her heart. "Mr. Herbert Harms, that's who."

"Herbert who?" July questioned.

"Come on, July. Remember I told you that Herbert Harms is Miss Smith's beau. AND ... he is coming after school tonight to propose." Celie spun in a circle. "Isn't it romantic? Let's hide after school and watch."

"I don't know." July hesitated. Everything inside of the girl told her it was wrong, but what a thing to see.

"Come on July," Celie begged. "We can hide behind the outhouse like we did before, and after Mr. Harms comes, we can sneak to a window and watch."

July liked Miss Smith, and if this made her happy, July was all for it. She would love to watch, but she could get in a batch of trouble. "I don't know ... maybe."

Celie took that for a "Yes" and twirled again, grabbing July's hand to swing together with hers.

At school, Franklin's hound jumped up and welcomed the girls with a wag of his tail.

Celie squealed and tried to run around him. "You stay way away from me, Mister." July laughed and scratched Moose behind the ears. The dog rolled and whined, begging for more. When it didn't come, he followed her into the school, and July thought she had made a friend forever.

Miss Smith threw up her hands. "Shoo, shoo. No dogs are allowed in school."

But Moose didn't shoo. He flopped down in front of July as she took her new seat beside Celie. Miss Smith clapped her hands, but Moose didn't budge. "Franklin, you will have to take your dog outside, and tell him not to come back in," Miss Smith instructed.

Some students stifled giggles, but all the kids had strayed from their work and were watching. Franklin tilted his head and grinned.

"Ahh, Miss Smith, Moose just knows a good thing when he sees it." Franklin reached down to latch onto his hound and then winked at July.

A loud *kerwhack* startled everyone. Prissy had dropped her slate to the hardwood floor. "Oops, I am so sorry, Miss Smith." Prissy's voice was syrupy as she stepped from her desk. That was when July noticed that Prissy's seat had been pushed to the corner in front of the class, and she worked alone. Prissy picked up her slate and flashed it at July. Only two words were written on the slate: AT LUNCH!

July didn't think she could handle another lunch like yesterday, but when lunch time arrived, Miss Smith rang a small bell on her desk. "It is lunch break. All of you, except Prissy, may gather your lunches and go outside. Prissy, you may eat at your desk. I will share my lunch with you."

Through stiff lips Prissy answered, "Yes, ma'am." But her eyes were glued on July.

Celie giggled as she and July went out the door. "I saw Prissy's note on her slate. I would say you were saved by the bell!"

And this lunch without Prissy was much better than yesterday's. It was wonderful.

6

The Proposal

AFTER school, July and Celie planned to walk toward home, then duck around the block and sneak back to the school. But Levi, Franklin, and Moose came running up behind them. The girls slowed to let them pass. The boys and Moose slowed, too. The girls sped up. The boys and Moose sped up.

Celie turned. "You keep following us. What are you guys trying to do?"

Levi laughed. "We are keeping you safe like detectives do. Didn't you watch Prissy follow you out the door?"

"No," Celie answered.

"She did?" July asked.

"She did, and she shook her fist at you," Levi said.

Franklin added, "That was when Miss Smith stepped out and told Prissy that her home was the other way, and she had better head for it, or her mother would come looking for her."

Levi smothered a laugh. "That is when Prissy tried to spit, but it landed on her chin. Franklin and I both saw it and started heehawing. Then Prissy dropped her empty black-eyed pea bowl, wiped her chin and yelled, 'I can take the both of you!'"

Levi wiped his forehead in relief. "The teacher saved us. She reminded Prissy again where home was, and Miss Smith stood and watched her go."

July swallowed. Even the orphanage school hadn't been this bad. Sometimes there were fights, but not that often. Of course, all the kids had been pretty well supervised all the time.

Levi stuck his thumb in his chest. "So, Franklin and I decided to be your bodyguards."

Celie wrinkled her nose. "We don't need any bodyguards, especially not guards with a dog."

Moose seemed to know he was being talked about and wagged his tail. Franklin reached down and grabbed a hunk of skin and shook it with affection. "Celie, he's a hound dog, and he can smell out the enemy. Moose doesn't like Prissy 'cause she's mean to him. He'll point and let you know if Prissy gets within smelling distance." Franklin shrugged. "And besides, Moose already likes July."

"So?" Celie snapped.

Franklin patted Moose. "It means he'll look out for July, and you if you're with July. He's a good ol' hound."

Celie spread her hands in frustration. "Look, Prissy is not in sight, so she isn't a threat anymore. July and I can get along without the three of you right now. So why don't you leave us to get on home alone. Besides, we have girl talk you don't even want to hear."

"Suit yourselves." Levi shrugged. "Come on Franklin. We got better things to do anyway."

July and Celie watched the boys and Moose go on ahead and around the corner. They heard Levi say, "I don't need any more girl talk. I get it at home all the time."

Celie grabbed July's hand. "Now's our chance. Come on, July, let's go fast. I want to see this whole thing."

Together they flew to the schoolyard and behind the outhouse just in time. Miss Smith's beau, carrying a bouquet of daisies tied with yellow ribbon, whistled as he walked around the other side of the school. In one lithe step, he was on the porch knocking at the school door. Miss Smith pulled the door wide, letting sunshine flood her face. A gentle blush followed. July thought that Miss Smith was beautiful and that her smile lit her eyes like candles on a Christmas tree.

"Am I too late for lessons, Miss Smith?" her beau asked, presenting the flowers to her.

Miss Smith giggled. "Herbert, they are gorgeous, and daisies are my favorite. How did you know?"

"Your mother told me, but they're not nearly as gorgeous as you are, Amanda." Mr. Harms leaned down and gave Miss Smith a sweet kiss on the lips.

Celie started fanning herself. "July, July, July! Did you see that? I've never even seen my mama and daddy kiss like that."

July slammed her finger to her lips and hissed, "Quiet."

Celie nodded.

Mr. Harms swirled Miss Smith in a circle and through the door, closing it behind them.

Celie began counting. When she reached fifty, she yanked July's arm. "Come on. Let's get to the window before we miss something important."

They tore across the playground to the front window. Celie was barely tall enough to see through the opening. She seized a good-sized rock and rolled it underneath the window while July peeked inside. Celie planted her feet on the rock and silently began her eaves-dropping.

In the cool of the schoolhouse, Mr. Harms sat on the edge of the teacher's desk. He held Miss Smith's hands. "Amanda, I can hardly live without you. When I am plowing behind the horses, all I can think of is you. When I work at Dad's furniture store, I cannot concentrate on anything but you. Customers have to ask me things at least twice before I can comprehend what they are saying. Thoughts of you have permeated my very being, and I love you so much. Amanda, I don't think I can live without you."

Miss Smith whispered, and the girls strained to hear. "Herbert, I love you, too. If it were not for the hope of seeing you, I don't know if I would be able to make it through this school year. It has been a couple of very tough days. Prissy Overton has been in a rage, and I know I must keep her away from July. I feel sorry for July because no matter what she does, Prissy is ready to fight her. July's grandfather has assured me he will help all he can, but Prissy's mother threatens to go to the school board and get me fired. Prissy's father is the banker, Jud Overton, and he is also the school board president."

"Amanda, I have a solution to your problem and mine." Gently he slipped from the desk to the floor on one knee. "Marry me, Amanda. Leave all this behind and marry me."

Miss Smith gasped. "I need to finish the year. I signed a contract, and I gave my word. But when this year is over, you bet I'll marry you."

Mr. Harms sprung from the floor, took Miss Smith in his arms and kissed her. Celie had covered her mouth, and July thought it was a good thing because Celie was likely to drool.

"Well, I never!" Mrs. Overton stood in the back of the school-room clutching Prissy's hand in hers.

Mr. Harms dropped his arms from about Miss Smith, and both whirled about to face the fiery Mrs. Overton. She had turned Prissy around to block her view of the couple and now had her hands over Prissy's ears.

"Miss Smith! What kind of an example are you to the children you teach?" Mrs. Overton screeched. "I already had concerns about the unjust treatment you have subjected Priscilla to in this classroom. You really think it's fair for her to sit at the front of the room to be made fun of by the rest of the class?" Mrs. Overton continued, "And now ... now this inappropriate behavior? I tell you I will not have it."

Miss Smith struggled to respond calmly. "Mrs. Overton, what I do in my classroom when there are no students is my affair. And if you notice, there are no students, except for your own child, whom you brought in without bothering to knock on my door."

"Miss Smith, the school is a public building, and I was not aware that the public must need knock before they enter," Mrs. Overton raged. "I hold you responsible for what my Priscilla has seen, bless her heart, and I pray it hasn't planted visions in her mind that she will not be able to forget." Mrs. Overton still held her daughter's ears.

Mr. Harms placed himself between the two ladies. "Mrs. Overton, please accept my apology. If any of the actions were inappropriate, it was my fault. Please don't blame Amanda."

Mrs. Overton glared. "I should think you would refer to our teacher as 'Miss Smith.' First names are inappropriate when students are present."

Mr. Harms grinned, and July thought he was mischievous, yet handsome at the same time. "Well, Mrs. Overton, I am hoping to make Amanda, 'Mrs. Herbert Harms.' I was also hoping to ask her without an audience, but since you are here, please enjoy." Herbert reached into his pocket and pulled out a delicate box. "Amanda, this is for you if you will have it."

Miss Smith's hand shook as she took the box, opened it, and soaked in the beauty of the ring. "Herbert, it is beautiful, and yes, oh, yes, I will marry you."

At that, Herbert drew Amanda into his arms again, and with a smile, kissed her right on the lips in front of Mrs. Overton.

"Of all the nerve. You can count your job gone, Missy." Mrs. Overton flounced toward the door, but turned to sputter, "This example for the children is inexcusable."

Before she could think of what she wanted to say, Mr. Harms lifted his head and winked at the hot-headed woman. "Mrs. Overton, your child is the only one in view, and you chose to keep her here. I would say you are the one submitting her to this scene."

"You brassy … " Mrs. Overton stammered as she turned to walk out the door.

That was when Levi and Franklin, who had followed the girls, keeping from sight as good detectives will, decided they had waited long enough. On tip-toes they slyly crept up behind the girls. Then they bellowed and charged July and Celie, grabbing them from behind and tumbling to the ground. Screams of horror deafened the ears of all those around. Mr. Harms and Miss Smith rushed to the window.

Miss Smith held her hand over her heart. All four kids were on their backs in the dry grass. Moose was licking Celie's face, and Celie was trying to push him away. Miss Smith worriedly asked, "Is everyone all right?" After a moment's pause, she added, "And how long have you all been at my window?"

Mrs. Overton was the one to answer as she shoved between Miss Smith and Mr. Harms to survey the children outside. "I will bet it has been long enough to watch the whole sordid scene, Miss Floosy. And you said no student would see you. The school board is definitely going to hear all about this, I assure you," Mrs. Overton hissed.

As she crossed to Prissy and yanked her arm, Mrs. Overton ordered, "Don't look, Priscilla," but Priscilla was getting an eyeful.

July had had enough of Prissy's mother. She marched into the schoolroom and declared, "It was not sordid. It was romantic and beautiful, but you probably wouldn't recognize romantic and beautiful." Without waiting for a response, July turned and stormed back out the door.

All the way home, the turmoil in July's tummy rolled. Ahead of her, Franklin and Levi gloated over scaring the girls, and Celie was unsuccessfully trying to dodge Moose. July wondered to herself,

Would Mrs. Overton go to the school board? Would she demand that Miss Smith lose her teaching job? Again her tummy rolled. She slowed as the church came into view. Gramps always had answers, and maybe she could catch him there. Without a word to the others, she walked toward the steps.

"Hey, July?" Celie bounced to her side. "What are you doing?"

"I want to talk to Gramps," July said.

"Want me to come with you?" Celie asked.

July just shrugged her shoulders, watching the boys fade in the distance with Moose bounding at their heels.

"Are you all right?" Celie whispered.

"I guess so, but I am worried about Miss Smith. She is the nicest teacher ever, and she didn't do a thing to Mrs. Overton. I don't know if Mrs. Overton can get her fired, and I want to talk to Gramps about it," July explained. "Gramps will know what to do, and he always makes me feel better."

Celie reached over and grabbed her hand. "I'll come with you."

Solemnly they walked up the steps and onto the porch. They stood frozen in the wide-open doorway, unnoticed. Gramps was already talking to someone, or rather listening to someone. Mrs. Overton had beat them to Gramps.

"I tell you right now, I will not have that floosy teaching my child! And I would think you would feel the same way as you, yourself have two granddaughters and a grandson exposed to her. Why, there is no telling what damage she has done already to their tender minds," Mrs. Overton ranted.

"Mrs. Overton, let's calm down. What happened?" Gramps was every bit the Pastor.

"They kissed! Right in front of my Priscilla, and I believe your granddaughters witnessed it, too," she huffed.

Confused, Gramps asked, "Who kissed?"

"Miss Smith and that Harms boy she has been seeing," Mrs. Overton retorted.

"Herbert Harms?" A smile flickered across Gramps's face.

"That's the one all right." Mrs. Overton was indignant.

"This was during school hours?" Gramps asked.

"No." Mrs. Overton took a deep breath before continuing. "But it is still unacceptable, and I am demanding a school board meeting right here tonight as soon as I can get everyone together."

"Mrs. Overton, are you requesting to use our church building for this meeting tonight?" Gramps asked.

Mrs. Overton drew her brows together. "I thought I made that clear. We need to meet as soon as possible to get this situation under control. Monday morning is coming all too soon."

"As is Sunday." Gramps sighed.

"What?" Mrs. Overton was puzzled.

Gramps smiled. "Seven tonight. I'll be here."

"Good." Mrs. Overton pulled herself straight, dismissing Gramps, and turned and strutted down the aisle.

Celie and July scattered from her path, but not before Mrs. Overton settled her glare on them. She narrowed her eyes and shook her finger. "Peeking through windows and eavesdropping are both sins. If I were you two, I would march in that church and fall to my knees." She grabbed Prissy's hand. "We have people to see, and stay away from those girls, Priscilla," she ordered as they walked away.

Gramps followed Mrs. Overton out and wearily watched her begin her mission. When she was out of earshot, he turned to the girls. "Can I help you young ladies?"

Celie's face held panic. July's held anger. "Why did you let her insist on having that meeting to fire Miss Smith here in your church?" she demanded.

"Whoa." Gramps knelt on one knee, taking a hand from each of the girls. "First, it is not my church. It belongs to the Lord. Second, if we have this meeting in God's house, He will be in charge of it, and I will be speaking for Him. Third, I feel the Lord would have us to start the school board meeting tonight with a good old-fashioned prayer meeting, and that can be done without question in God's house, God's territory."

July's eyes glistened with unshed tears. "Thank you, Gramps. Miss Smith is so nice to me. Please make them be nice to her."

"We'll do better than that. We will pray God will make them be nice to her." He paused. "Girls, I believe I might drop by Miss Smith's house and make sure she knows of this meeting tonight. We wouldn't want any surprises. While I do that, why don't you and Celie run tell Grams I'll be a little late for supper."

Both girls hugged their gramps and scrambled down the steps. July turned and blew a first-time kiss to her gramps. He always made her feel safe and warm and calm. She knew the meeting would go well because it was in good hands.

That evening, July came downstairs—for the third time—to get a drink. She was supposed to be in bed, and she knew she was pushing Grams's patience with the continued trips to the kitchen, but she had to know how the meeting went. Before she reached the bottom step, she could hear Gramps talking with Grams. "...so despite Mildred's fervent attempt to have Miss Smith fired, the school board would not agree with her." July didn't need to hear any more. Miss Smith would still be her teacher. July ran back upstairs and crawled happily in to bed, glad that she had Gramps—and God—to fight her battles.

7

The Wedding

ON Sunday morning, July sat at the kitchen table eating a sandwich of toast and garden tomatoes. She thought fresh tomatoes were one of the best things she had ever tasted. When she put them on toast, she could eat a bellyful. They were another first for her. July couldn't remember ever having tomatoes before. Through the summer she had helped Grams take care of the garden, popping cherry tomatoes in her mouth as they worked. She liked to feel them squirt when she bit into them. It sure made garden work fun.

She watched Gramps walk into the kitchen in his Sunday suit, step close to Grams, circle his arms about her and softly ask, "Pretty lady, would you be kind enough to tie my tie?" Then he gave her a butterfly kiss right on the lips.

Grams's hands were on his shoulders in no time to push him away as she scolded, "Ezra, July is watching."

July blushed.

Gramps looked over Grams's shoulder and winked at his granddaughter. "July needs to know that when married people love each other they show it no matter how old they are." Before Grams could stop him, he kissed her again.

Grams pushed him away with a giggle. "Tie your own tie, young man."

"But you do it so much better." He laughed.

"All right. Stick your hands in your pockets," Grams ordered with a chuckle.

Gramps grinned, but he obeyed. He shoved his hands into his pockets, and Grams tied his tie. At the door Gramps grabbed his hat. "I'm going on to the church to take care of some last minute things, and I don't want two of my favorite ladies to be late. It's going to be a great day," he said.

"We'll be there," Grams assured him.

July mumbled something around a huge mouthful of toast and tomatoes.

The September day was blown with soft winds. Leaves still grasped tightly to their trees, even though they flushed with pastel colors. July skipped alongside Grams as they headed to the church.

The church house was packed, and July was glad Aunt Sybil had saved them a place. She was also glad she didn't have to sit by Aunt Sybil or Levi. As it was, Levi and Franklin were right behind her, so she would have to watch out. Franklin was okay, but Levi was walking, or rather sitting trouble.

"July, I'm so excited," Celie said.

"About church?" July asked.

"No, silly, about Miss Smith and Mr. Harms."

July tipped her head to the side. "What about Miss Smith and Mr. Harms?" Gramps had told July and Celie that the school board had not fired Miss Smith during the meeting Friday night, so she couldn't guess what Celie could be so excited about.

Celie sat straighter. "You don't know?" she asked eagerly.

July raised her eyebrows and leaned toward Celie. "Does it look like I know?"

"But I thought you would. After all, Gramps met with them last night to make the plans. Mama told me what they were doing."

"Plans?" July asked curiously.

"To get married. Today after services," said Celie.

"Your mama told you that?" July asked.

Celie responded hesitantly. "Well, sort of. I heard her telling my dad."

"Celie, that's eavesdropping. Someday you're going to get into big trouble," July warned.

"Maybe, but at least I'm informed. Our very own Miss Smith is getting married right here after Gramps preaches," Celie gushed, her legs swinging from the pew in anticipation.

"So, that's why Grams and Gramps were so smoochie this morning," July responded as she reflected on the events at breakfast.

Levi grabbed the back of the pew and pulled his face close to whisper in July's ear. "Smoochie? Franklin would like … "

But before he could finish the words, July shoved her nose next to his. "Don't even say it, Levi. I promise I will punch both your eyes black and blue," she threatened.

Levi snickered. "Like your black eye?" Then he scooted quickly to the back of his pew to stay out of her reach.

The church service began, and July sang all of the hymns. She had learned most of them through the summer, and sometimes she even sang or hummed them while working in the garden or around the house. She liked the hymns because they were a part of her new home, and she felt the songs were peaceful like Grams and Gramps. Most of her time here had been peaceful—well, maybe not. There was Levi and Prissy. And Prissy? She wouldn't miss a wedding for the world … if she knew about the wedding. July rather thought Prissy's mom knew everything that happened in Plevna, so Mrs. Overton definitely would be here. Surely Prissy had to be here, too.

"And God said … " Gramps declared as he slapped the wooden pulpit. At the same time, Levi kicked the pew beneath her. July jumped. Swiftly she swung her head around, piercing Levi with a warning glare. His big-toothed smile proved that the kick was no accident. July turned back to Gramps, but there was no way she could settle her mind to concentrate on Gramps's message today. It was then that she spied Prissy's mother in a bright green hat, and there was Prissy right beside her. July was right. They must have known about the wedding, too, because July hadn't seen them at church before.

"Amen." Gramps closed his prayer. He then held up his hand and announced, "We are not done here yet. Today we have the great honor and privilege to witness the wedding of one of our very own: Miss Amanda Smith. Last night I met with Amanda and her young man, Mr. Herbert Harms from over in Hudson. They have assured me that they both know the Lord Jesus Christ as their Savior, and they feel it is in His will for them to marry. Both sets of parents agree, and we are most happy to have all the family in our services today. Having thus said, Herbert would you come on up here, and then we will have Amanda's father bring her up the aisle."

Herbert was ready to burst with pride. There was a rustle from the back as Amanda and her father stepped into the aisle. Miss Smith was radiant in a light blue dress flowing just below her knees. A wide yellow ribbon wound through her dark-brown curls, and July thought she looked beautiful.

Celie nudged July. "That's what I want to look like when I get married."

July closed her eyes and whispered, "Me, too."

Mrs. Overton swooped to her feet. "I have an objection," she shrilled.

Gramps cleared his throat and smiled as he said, "Great idea, Mrs. Overton. Everyone please stand as the bride and her father come down the aisle."

"What?" Mrs. Overton's question was drowned out by all the clutter of noise made as people stood to their feet.

When the bride and her father were front and center, Gramps continued, "Thank you. You may all be seated."

Everyone sat except Mrs. Overton. "Pastor, I object to this wedding. This is a church, a holy place, and this woman is a deplorable example for our children. As you know, she was asked to resign her teaching position because of unladylike conduct in front of even your own granddaughter. Pastor, I don't think she should have a church wedding. If they want to get married, they can go to the justice of the peace, but they should not be getting married in 'our' church," Mrs. Overton insisted.

Gasps twittered over the congregation, and Gramps raised his hand to quiet them as he spoke in a calm voice. "Mrs. Overton, it is good to see you here in our church. I think it's been all summer since we last saw you here. I want you to understand, Mrs. Overton, the membership of *our* church is not so easily swayed as the school board. We believe the Holy Book teaches forgiveness. In First Peter 4:8 God says, 'And above all things have fervent charity among yourselves: for charity shall cover the multitude of sins.' We all know charity means love, and covering a multitude of sins means forgiveness. Love is to forgive."

Mrs. Overton huffed. "The things Miss Smith has done need to have a hardy answer from God's people. Her display in front of innocent children is unforgivable."

July was shaking all over, and she had had enough. What Mrs. Overton had said and was saying about Miss Smith was all wrong. She had to do something or she felt she would burst. July jumped up and latched onto the pew in front of her to steady herself as she blurted, "Gramps, Miss Smith has been a fine example to me. She stood for what was right, even when she had been threatened with her job, and I think that is noble." July took a deep breath and continued, "I hope I can grow up to be just like Miss Smith."

Silence settled, and a smile played at Gramps's lips. "Thank you, July. I don't know how many times I have said, 'out of the mouth of babes,' yet it never ceases to amaze me. Brothers and Sisters in Christ, we could learn from our own children. In fact, I think our Heavenly Father would want us to," Gramps declared.

Mrs. Overton shook her head. "Pastor, you cannot mean you are going through with this ceremony! And just because your granddaughter, from who knows where, says Miss Smith is a good example?" she asked incredulously.

July could tell Gramps was swallowing a bunch of things he would like to say and turning the other cheek before calmly responding. "Yes, Mrs. Overton, that is exactly what we are going to do. If you do not feel you can be a part of this wedding, I'm sure Miss Smith and Mr. Harms will be pleased to excuse you."

Mrs. Overton threw her hand over her heart. "Well, I never! Come, Priscilla. Let's leave."

"But, Mother, I want to see the wedding," Prissy whined.

"No, we will not be a part of this charade. We are going," Mrs. Overton snapped as she clutched her pocketbook in one hand and her daughter's arm in the other. She dragged both behind her as she squeezed through the people in her pew and marched down the aisle. When they passed July, Prissy glared, but July could see the glassy haze of tears in her eyes. For the first time, July felt sorry for the girl.

The church doors slammed behind them, and silence settled over the room. July thought it was rather like the verse Gramps had quoted, only instead of 'charity shall cover a multitude of sins,' it would read, 'silence shall cover a multitude of sins.' Maybe silence had a lot to do with charity? July decided she would have to ask Gramps that question later.

"Now, if there is anyone else who would like to be dismissed, you may feel free to go," Gramps offered.

No one seemed to even breathe.

"Good ... let me gather my thoughts. Oh yes, who gives this bride?" Gramps asked.

Miss Smith paused to glance to her groom before she stepped over and whispered something in Gramps's ear. July watched him smile and nod. The bride turned and swished back down the aisle. She stopped at July's pew and whispered, "July, sweetie, thank you. That was one of the nicest things anyone has ever done for me. Would you come be my flower girl?"

"Me?" July asked in amazement.

Miss Smith smiled. "Yes, you."

With wide eyes, July looked across Celie to Grams. Celie was glowing. Grams nodded, and July thought she saw a tear ready to spill.

July whispered, "But I don't have any flowers. Don't you have to have flowers to be a flower girl?"

Miss Smith always had a solution. She knelt on the floor, laid her bouquet on the hard wood and untied the yellow ribbon which held the daisies together. She plucked a handful of the daisies from the spray of flowers and handed them to July. Then she took the yellow ribbon, and instead of tying her bouquet back together, she twisted it through July's short, wild curls. Miss Smith held her hand to July, and together they walked back up the aisle toward the beaming groom, yellow ribbons flowing.

July felt like crying, but she would not. Instead, she proudly held the bouquet in one hand and placed her other hand over her mama's ring hanging from the golden chain about her neck.

The Sad Goodbye

CELIE cut through the tree row running. She grabbed July and hid behind her. "Keep him away from me!"

July didn't have to ask who because Moose burst through the trees and made a beeline for Celie. "You don't have to be scared, Celie." July laughed. "He's just a dog, and he likes you."

"He's a big dog. He smells like a dog, and I don't like him," Celie said.

July knelt and scooped Moose's head in her hands. She rubbed the extra skin behind his ears. "Moose, Celie wants you to stay away from her. She thinks you are too big and stinky," July murmured softly.

"Ahh, Moose ain't stinky. He just smells like a dog," Franklin said as he and Levi strolled up behind the girls.

"That is because he is a dog, Franklin." Celie shrugged.

"You got good eyes." Franklin laughed at his own joke, and Levi joined in.

"Very funny," Celie retorted. She tried not to laugh, but when she saw July's hand slapped over her mouth hiding a snicker, Celie joined in.

Franklin reasoned, "And maybe it's not you he likes so much as what you got in your lunch."

Celie made a face. "Moose likes peanut butter and jelly sandwiches?"

Franklin nodded. "Mostly Moose eats anything that can't get away from him, but peanut butter and jelly would be at the top of his list, right up there with dead mice."

Like a flash Celie fished in her lunch bag and threw Moose a chunk of sandwich. "Now, stay away from me," she commanded.

The dog gulped the bite of peanut butter and jelly sandwich and wagged his tail, begging for more.

"Moose wants my whole sandwich, doesn't he?" Celie asked.

Moose whined while inching closer to the girl.

"You said that would work," Celie accused.

"It should have." Franklin frowned.

By now, Moose was even closer, and Celie was beginning to panic.

"Stay, Moose, stay," Franklin ordered.

But Moose whined and started toward Celie. Celie backed away. Moose followed. Celie couldn't stand it anymore. She swirled about and ran. The hound loped after her. Celie looked over her shoulder with horror and sped faster. At the school, she scrambled up the steps and dove for the door, but it was still closed firmly. Celie swung around and plastered her back against the door, only to find she was nose to nose with the dog. Foamy spit dribbled from the sides of his mouth and slung down the front of her dress. Wide-eyed and trembling, she threw her whole lunch past him, hoping Franklin was right, and that Moose was after it and not her. It worked. Moose cleared the steps in one bound and was gobbling the rest of the lunch, paper and all. With relief, Celie bent over and clutched her ankles.

Franklin whistled. "You can really run for a girl."

July added, "I think she's every bit as fast as Levi."

"She is not," Levi argued.

Celie sunk to the top step and sat. "Moose ate my whole lunch. You need to leave that dog at home, Franklin," she insisted.

"Not a chance," Franklin declared. "Moose and me, we're part-ners. Where I go, he goes." Franklin sat on the bottom step and patted the side of his leg to motion for his partner. Moose moseyed over, stretched, yawned, and flopped to ground at his partner's feet. "See, partners."

"Well, your partner ate my lunch," Celie complained.

"You can have mine." Franklin handed her a tied oil cloth.

Celie sniffed it. "It smells pretty good. What's in it?"

Mischief radiated from Franklin's eyes as he drawled, "Fried hog jowl and pone bread."

Celie turned a shade of green. Levi rolled on the ground with laughter. "Celie eating hog jowl. I got to see this," he teased.

July came to her rescue. "Celie, I'll share mine with you."

Behind them, the school door opened and Miss Smith, or rather Mrs. Harms, rang the bell.

Surprised and delighted, students flooded into the school to take their seats, all except for Prissy. She stood tall as she cut through her peers and walked right up to Mrs. Harms. "I thought the school board fired you."

Most of the kids held their breath. No one talked to the teacher with disrespect like that and got by with it. Calmly Mrs. Harms addressed her student. "Prissy, please take your seat."

Prissy shook her head. "My mother said I didn't have to sit up in front of every one. She said that was unjustified punishment, and I don't think you can make me since you were fired," Prissy boldly replied.

Mrs. Harms and Prissy stood almost face to face. "Prissy, I really don't care where you sit. In fact, if you would like to leave and come back later, that would be fine," Mrs. Harms said.

Prissy was startled, but she backed away and turned to find an empty seat.

"Thank you, Prissy," Mrs. Harms said. She stepped to her desk and caressed the wood. Then she turned and explained with a wistful smile, "It is true. I am no longer your teacher. I am sure most of your parents have informed you. However, the school board did not ask for my resignation. They did reprimand my actions, but they were kind enough to give me an hour with my students. This is my hour." She looked at the small watch pinned to her blouse. "And time is passing quickly."

Prissy raised her hand.

"Yes, Prissy?" Mrs. Harms asked patiently.

"If the school board didn't fire you, then how come you are leaving?" Prissy inquired smugly.

Their teacher nodded. "That is a fair enough question, Prissy. The school board asked about the plans Mr. Harms and I had made. They would have liked for me to finish the school term as I agreed to under the contract that I had signed. When my husband asked me to marry him, we had planned to wait to get married until school was finished in May."

Prissy interrupted, "Then why aren't you staying to finish the year?"

"My husband had an opportunity to buy some farm land a bit east of Garden City. Both he and I feel it would be detrimental to our marriage if I stayed here and he went there. We made the decision together. I am going with him," she announced.

Franklin asked what most everyone in the class wanted to know. "What does *detrimental* mean?"

Their teacher laughed. "I should make you get the dictionary and look it up, but this is my last bit of time with you, so I am choosing to let it slide."

Most of the students were a part of the "yay" which spread over the room.

Mrs. Harms smiled. "I am going to miss all of you."

"Even Prissy?" someone from the back asked.

"Who said that?" Prissy asked.

Silence followed, and no one would admit to saying it, mainly because most of them were afraid of Prissy.

Mrs. Harms cleared her throat. "*Detrimental* means destructive or harmful. Both Mr. Harms and I thought it would be destructive or harmful to our marriage if we chose to live half way across the state from each other."

Franklin chimed in, "That's why no one will admit to asking if you were sorry to leave Prissy behind. It would be detrimental to their health."

All the class laughed except Prissy and Mrs. Harms, who very delicately put her handkerchief over her mouth to hide a suspicious cough.

Prissy stood with her hands on her hips. "I will find out who said that, and it WILL be detrimental."

Mrs. Harms clapped her hands to get her students' attention. "All of you have learned your vocabulary lesson very well for today. I trust no one will forget our new word. Now, are there any other questions?" she asked.

Celie raised her hand. "Do we have another teacher?"

"Yes, but she cannot come until the change of semesters. She is obligated until January the third," Mrs. Harms replied.

Levi slapped his leg. "Yahoo! This is only September, and we will be out of school until January the third. Thank you, Mrs. Harms."

"Oh, Levi, I will miss you." Mrs. Harms laughed. "The school board has assured me they have found a qualified teacher who has agreed to come out of retirement and fill in the rest of this term."

"Rats," Levi and others with the same sentiment groaned.

Mrs. Harms continued, "I want you all to promise that you will be nice to this older lady. I'm sure she retired for a good reason, so she will be needing your full cooperation. That means I want you to be on your very best behavior. Does everyone understand?"

A combined, "Yes, Miss Smith and Yes, Mrs. Harms," flowed over the room.

"Good. Now if there are no other questions, I have a surprise for you. Anyone?" she asked.

Silence settled over the room. All were ready for a surprise.

Again, Mrs. Harms looked at her watch. "We have twenty-seven minutes left, and I baked sugar cookies for a 'got married' party. I'll stand at the door; each of you can get a cookie, and we'll spend the rest of our time together on the playground."

All of the students clapped and cheered.

Sorrow tugged at July's heart as she stared at her cookie. Mrs. Harms had been an ally in the war zone of the classroom. She was a friend in deed, and July was going to miss her. She bit into the huge cookie, savoring the crunch of sugar sprinkles. The sweet flavor would forever bring to mind Mrs. Harms.

"I'm going to miss her," Celie mumbled around a small bite of cookie. "July, if you take little bites, the cookie will last longer."

"I am," July answered. "I want Mrs. Harms to last a long time." July closed her eyes to print her teacher forever in her mind.

Celie took another tiny bite. "Mrs. Harms makes a good cookie, and she sure made them big."

Moose was trotting towards the two girls when July opened her eyes. "Celie!" July's warning was almost too late.

Celie turned to look behind her. She jumped to her feet. "Oh no you don't, Moose Mange!" Celie crammed the rest of the cookie into her mouth. She slammed her lips tight just as the hound sprung and planted his paws on her shoulders. Then Moose swiped his tongue across her lips.

Franklin yanked his dog away, but he was laughing. "Celie, I think Moose is sweet on you. He likes July to pet him, but he likes anything you eat. You sure made yourself a friend."

"Way to go, Celie." Levi chuckled.

Celie glared, but she didn't say a word. Her mouth was so full of sugar cookie she could hardly chew.

The bell rang, and students lined up to go inside. Celie and July were last because Celie was still chewing.

Mrs. Harms was hugging and giving a light kiss on the cheek to each student as they passed through the door. July watched as Levi and Franklin shied away a bit, but they blushed with an impish grin as they accepted the hug and kiss. She watched as her teacher even hugged and kissed the rigid Prissy. July tried not to cry, but the harder she tried, the more she knew a cloud burst was about to strike right here in the middle of the drought in Plevna, Kansas.

July was at the end of the line. Mrs. Harms took her blue-flow-ered handkerchief to pat July's cheeks. "Honey, I want you to be strong and never give up. You have strength in your character, and God has given you a wonderful family. Always remember the Lord. He will see you through anything He allows in your path," Mrs. Harms encouraged.

July could only nod.

"You are very special, Miss June July Calendar. When we have children, I may name my little girl, July. Would that be fine?" Mrs. Harms asked.

July wrapped her arms around her teacher and sobbed. When she pulled away, Mrs. Harms was crying, too. Gently she whispered, "You had best go to class now, Miss July." She pushed the girl through the door, and very quietly added, "I love you, July. Be strong."

July looked at the floor. She didn't want the other students to catch her crying. It wasn't their business. She slid into her seat beside Celie on the front row.

The classroom was quieter than she ever had heard it. Celie mysteriously whispered, "It will be fine. It's only until January third."

"What?" July looked at Celie with confusion.

But Celie didn't have time to answer. A wooden stick rapped the top of July's desk. "My first rule: There will be no talking."

July's heart began chugging as loud as the train that had brought her to this place surging uphill. July didn't have to look up to know who the new teacher was. She would know that voice anywhere. She felt a lump form in her heart. What would she do now?

"Am I understood, Miss Calendar?" the new teacher demanded.

July straightened her shoulders. Mrs. Harms must have known. She had told her to be strong and remember the Lord.

The teacher bellowed, "I am waiting. Rule number two: Always answer the teacher."

July threw her head back and answered, "Yes, ma'am, Mrs. Drunyon."

9

The Return of the Dragon

"**CHILDREN,** you will have precisely one hour for lunch. I will be inside, and I expect to be left alone unless there is a dire emergency." With little emotion, Mrs. Drunyon continued her instructions. "While you are on your break, you will eat your lunch and take care of your business. We will not be wasting class time for your personal needs. When the hour is up, I will blow my whistle at which time you will immediately line up in single file. Then we will begin class."

Mrs. Drunyon had not seen Moose lounging to the side of the door. He stood and stretched his tongue. He then stuck his nose under the edge of Mrs. Drunyon's skirt to offer a dog's friendly "hello." To further his sniffing exploration, Moose shoved his cold, wet nose against her leg and slid his tongue over her kneecap. Mrs. Drunyon jumped higher than orthopedic shoes should allow. She screamed and wildly danced a jig across the porch. Skirts and dog hair flew. Moose yelped and dove in all directions, trying to get untangled from the frenzy of the savage, clomping feet. In desperation, he cowered down and crawled to the edge of the porch, dropped to the ground, and scooted underneath the floorboards until he was out of sight.

It was a laughing matter, but the kids were afraid to make a sound. Everyone stared at Mrs. Drunyon. With a humph, she straightened her skirts and patted her hair back in place as best as she could. She glared at the whole group before she declared, "There will be no dogs or pets of any kind allowed at school." She turned and stomped into the classroom, slamming the door behind her.

Slowly, the students found places around the schoolyard to partner and eat their lunches. Celie, Levi, Franklin, and July gathered close to the porch, but Moose refused to leave the safety he had found.

"At least I won't have to fight Moose for whatever lunch I get to eat today." Celie giggled.

"Poor Moose." July sympathized as she tossed a piece of biscuit under the porch.

Franklin winked at Celie. "I got plenty of fried hog jowl, you want some?"

Celie wrinkled her nose. "No, Franklin. I think you're the only one who ever brings that disgusting stuff to school in his lunch."

Franklin laughed. "I'd be happy to share; after all, you shared your lunch with my dog."

"Poor, poor, Moose," July moaned again. The dog whined, begging for more biscuit.

Levi looked toward the closed schoolhouse door. "Poor Moose, July? I'd say poor us."

"But I thought The Dragon left Plevna," Celie groaned. "Her house has been empty for a long time, ever since the shed incident."

"I wish she had gone to China. That's where dragons live," July stated.

"Dragons?" Franklin asked.

"Yep." Levi quit trying to coax Moose from his hideout and dropped to the ground. "That's what July calls her. I guess you could say July brought 'The Dragon' here in the first place," Levi claimed.

"You brought Mrs. Drunyon? Why did you do that, July?" Franklin asked.

Defeated, July responded, "I didn't bring her here. She brought me here."

"Why? Why did you bring her here? She scares the living daylights out of me, and you can see what she did to Moose." Franklin was full of questions.

July nodded her agreement. "She has that effect on most everybody I know, except Gramps. He has stood up to her before. I think that is because Gramps is close to God, so The Dragon doesn't get too close to him," July speculated.

Franklin laughed. "I guess we had all better be getting close to God then." Everyone chuckled at his humor. Franklin became serious. "July, do you really call her 'The Dragon'? And how do you know her?"

July handed Celie a biscuit sandwich before answering. "I don't call her The Dragon around Gramps, and mostly I try not to call her anything. And no one can know we call her The Dragon, or I will be in big trouble at home. Understand?" July looked to make sure all three of them understood.

Levi nodded. Celie agreed. "Cross my heart and hope to die," said Franklin.

July continued, "She worked at the orphanage I was in. One day someone in the office received information stating I had grandparents. After the office contacted Grams and Gramps and found out they wanted me, Mrs. Drunyon volunteered to escort me on the train here to Plevna."

"Why?" Franklin tipped his head in question.

"The Dragon is from here," said Levi.

"From Plevna?" Franklin asked.

"Yep," Levi assured him.

"I ain't never heard of her," Franklin muttered.

"Oh, you know her. Her husband is the famous Maxworth Drunyon," Levi informed Franklin.

"The bank robber?" asked Franklin. "Then it was true about our bank being robbed?"

Levi nodded. "Yep. It happened before we were born, and people don't talk about it much anymore."

"The Dragon's husband was Maxworth Drunyon, the bank robber," Franklin repeated in awe.

"Yep. That's the one. Only he was really a bank embezzler 'cause he didn't use a gun or anything. He used the bank books, his pen, and paper to take out thousands of dollars. And he was smart. He did it over a couple of years so no one would notice," Levi explained.

Franklin crunched his pone bread. "Did they ever find the money?"

Levi shook his head. "Nope. Not one single, solitary dime. And the police looked for it."

Franklin raised his eyebrow, "Maybe The Dragon has it stashed away somewhere."

"No," Celie answered.

"How do you know she doesn't?" Franklin asked.

Celie paused before answering. "Because we were hiding in her shed with old Maxworth Drunyon's black Model-T when she axed down the door and started talking to him." Celie shivered at the memory.

Franklin stopped chewing. "She axed down the door?"

Celie nodded. "She chopped down the door with an axe, and then she threw the axe into the wall above July's head."

"Whoa!" Franklin looked in awe at July and then turned back to Celie. "Wait. She was talking to Maxworth Drunyon? But isn't he dead?" Franklin asked.

Celie responded tensely, "Yes, he is dead, but that didn't stop her from talking to him. She wanted to know where he hid the money."

Levi lowered his voice and asked mysteriously, "Franklin, do you believe in ghosts?"

Franklin blinked as he thought for a moment. "Only when it's dark and windy. I'm not ever sure if it's really the wind, especially September winds. They have an eerie whine, and they seem to blow in death. The trees die, and the gardens die, and the flowers die, and the grass dies. By the end of September, most everything is dead, and if it's not, it's close to it."

"Dead? Well, nothing grows in that shed, that's for sure, especially around that old Model-T," Levi agreed.

Celie added with a shudder, "That shed gives me the willies just thinking about it."

"Then don't think about it, Celie," July suddenly blurted. She had been unusually quiet up until now, so her outburst startled Celie. July quickly looked over her shoulder. She could feel the thick presence of Maxworth and his Model-T running up her spine.

After pausing with thought, Franklin inquired, "Do you think the money is hidden somewhere in that shed, or even in his old Model-T?"

"Maybe," Levi responded with excitement at the thought.

"After school? Shall we go together after school and search?" Franklin asked.

Celie threw her hands over her mouth. "Oh … oh … oh … you can't do that. You've got to be crazy to even try that again, Levi," Celie insisted.

July now spoke calmly. "I think you both are crazy, but go ahead." She hastened to remind Levi, "Remember the last time? You couldn't get out of there fast enough. You said Maxworth whispered to you, and you could feel his ghost."

Levi shrugged. "This time I'll have Franklin with me. It'll be two men and not just me with a couple of scaredy-cat girls." He turned to Franklin. "After school?"

Franklin nodded. "After school, and we take Moose with us. Moose for sure doesn't believe in ghosts."

"Deal." Levi stuck his hand out for a shake.

Franklin spit in his hand, and Levi didn't think it was unsavory at all. He gripped Franklin's hand in his and grinned at July. "Guy spit. Man spit. Not girl goo."

July glared at him.

Celie spoke. "I still don't understand. The Dragon has been gone most of the summer. Where did she go, and why is she back?"

"Celie, why don't you walk right up to her and ask, 'Where were you all summer, Mrs. Drunyon?'" Levi challenged.

A shadow fell over the group. For fear it might be Mrs. Drunyon, everyone stopped talking and gingerly looked up. It was Prissy with her hands on her hips as she smugly offered, "I can tell you where she was, if you really want to know."

"Where?" they all asked at once.

Taking her time, Prissy joined the group and sat cross-legged on the grass. With a glamorous flip of her bobbed hair, she lowered her voice to say, "She was in Larned, Kansas at the State Hospital."

Levi gulped. "That's where they put crazy people."

Prissy corrected. "Sick people. It's impolite to call crazy people 'crazy.' We refer to them as sick people."

"How did she get out?" Celie demanded.

"Well, that's a silly question. Don't you think she was probably dismissed?" Prissy retorted.

Celie frowned. "You mean they said she was well?"

"Of course. There are only two ways you can get out of Larned State Hospital: get dismissed or die," Prissy told her. "So, I guess she is well."

Levi stuck his head forward and wagged it like a chicken. "Well? You didn't see The Dragon chop down a door with an axe."

Prissy raised her eyebrows. "The Dragon?"

July glared at Levi.

Levi spread his hands apologetically. "Sorry. It slipped."

Prissy sat back, crossed her arms and smiled. "'The Dragon,' I take it, is your name for Mrs. Drunyon," she smirked. "That is priceless. Isn't this a juicy tidbit of information? I am sure it is something Mrs. Drunyon would like to know. I think I will tuck that info away for future use … in case I need it." She turned to July. "Right, July? Do you understand who to stay away from?"

"Yes." July forced the word out through clenched teeth.

"Good." Prissy stood and walked away without glancing back.

After she was gone, July whispered, "I will stay away from you, Prissy, and The Dragon."

Moose lumbered out from beneath the porch and wagged his tail. Mrs. Drunyon stepped to the porch with her hands on her hips and her whistle in her lips. She stomped her foot and blew a long shrill sound that cut through the air. Moose yelped, wheeled around, and scrambled for his dark concealment again. Celie giggled.

"Poor, Moose," said July. "School is going to be hard for that dog."

Franklin smiled. "Oh, Moose will be fine. He's really a brave hound."

July turned to Franklin and laughed. "I can see that." She turned back to go inside the school and saw Prissy glaring menacingly.

Prissy mouthed the words, "I warned you."

July grabbed her lunch sack and headed for the line. She wondered about Gramps's 'turn the other cheek' lesson. *Just how many cheeks will I have to offer Prissy before this school year was over?*

From behind her, July heard Levi remind Franklin, "After school we make straight for The Dragon's place. She'll stick around here to grade papers, and we'll be safe."

"I'll bring Moose," Franklin said to add courage and comfort.

July threw over her shoulder, "Safe? Moose is going to protect you from The Dragon? I wouldn't count on it."

10

The Haunted Shed

"**FINE,** Celie and I will go along and let you know if we see The Dragon coming," July agreed as she and Celie followed Levi and Franklin. "But Celie and I will not go into that shed. We are only look-outs."

July picked up a rock and threw it, not at anything in particular. She watched it thud across the street as she thought about what a horrible day it had been. Mrs. Harms, her beloved teacher, had said goodbye. The Dragon, of all people, had taken her place, and Prissy was mad at July again for being a friend to Franklin. Life was hard at ten.

The boys had stopped at the back edge of Mrs. Drunyon's yard. Levi was pointing toward the 'haunted' shed, as the boys had decided to call it. "I think we can go in the door," Levi said.

Franklin squinted. "What door?"

Indicating an opening in the haunted shed, Levi explained, "There used to be a door there, and it was chained with a paddle lock. That was the door The Dragon axed to pieces."

"Jeepers, she's scary enough without an axe," Franklin said as he stared at the dark opening of the haunted shed.

July stopped behind them. "What are you waiting for? There is your haunted shed. No one is around, so this is your chance to explore. Celie and I will wait here and watch."

Nervously twisting the sides of her skirt with both hands, Celie urged, "You better hurry. This place gives me the creeps."

"Okay. Okay. We're going," Levi said. "Come on, Franklin. You can go first 'cause you haven't been in there before."

Franklin stopped in his tracks. "I'm not going first. You know where you're going, I don't. You go first."

July laughed. "I thought boys were brave."

Celie giggled. "Me, too."

Levi glared at July. "We men are brave. I was being polite to Franklin." He turned. "Come on, Franklin. We'll show them just how brave men are."

Franklin patted Moose on the head. "You stay here. You'll get in the way if you're with us."

Celie rolled her eyes. "Great. We get Moose. I don't know which is worse, this dog or the haunted shed."

"The haunted shed is worse, Celie, and you know it." July sat in the grass and coaxed Moose to her side. "Good boy." Celie sat on the other side of July to keep as far away from the hound as possible.

"You're wasting time, men," July taunted.

Levi glared then turned to Franklin. "Let's get this over with."

The two boys stealthily crossed to the shed and planted their backs against it. They slid along the side until they reached the opening. Levi held up one finger, then two fingers and then three. July laughed. So they were counting before they entered. Levi only had ten fingers, so they had to go in to the shed by the count of ten.

"What do you think they're waiting for?" Celie asked.

"I think they want to go in, but they don't want to go in. Levi really feels the shed is haunted by Maxworth's ghost," July explained.

Celie whispered, "Do you think it is haunted?"

July shrugged her shoulders. "It's creepy, but I don't know if it's haunted. I don't think of the shed as haunted when I'm not in there, but when I was in the shed, I could've believed it."

The boys must have reached ten because they disappeared inside the dark building.

Celie pulled a dandelion puff from the ground and blew the seeds to the sky. "July, did you think Prissy was being overly nice to Mrs. Drunyon today?" she asked.

"Yes. And it worked. She's not sitting in that chair in front of the class anymore." July sighed. "I think she wants to be the teacher's pet."

Celie thought about that. "I'll bet you're right. I sure wouldn't want to be The Dragon's pet."

"I don't think you'll have to worry about it. You're my cousin, and there's no way The Dragon will let you be her pet," July told Celie.

A cool wind rose and swept through the trees. Branches scratched against the side of the shed. Levi and Franklin suddenly burst out the door yelling, "What was that?"

July laughed. "Just the wind, men."

"Funny!" Levi growled.

Franklin cringed. "Levi, I don't like the wind when it sounds like ghosts moving around. It'll be fine with me if we do this later!"

"No. We're here, and The Dragon isn't. Now is the time to find that hidden money Maxworth Drunyon stashed away," Levi reasoned. "Besides, we've got to prove we're men."

Franklin slid his sweaty hands down the sides of his overalls. "Then let's get it done," he reluctantly agreed as they again disappeared inside the shed.

The girls lay back in the grass, and Moose stood to stretch. As he shook himself, dog drool sprayed the girls.

"Oh, ick! Dog spit," Celie shrieked as she took the edge of her skirt and wiped her cheek. "Get way away from me you mangy dog," Celie ordered.

July wrinkled her nose as she wiped her face, too. "You'll live, Celie. It's just dog slobbers."

"I hate dog slobbers. I don't know how you can stand it. Go on, Moose Mange, get out of here!" Celie shouted.

Moose moseyed to the middle of the yard and stopped to sniff some treasure he had found. July watched while Moose licked his new find. "I think Moose has found a dead bird," she told Celie.

"He had better stay away from me." Celie scrambled to her feet.

Moose gulped then suddenly pricked his ears and held his tail straight out. A bang blasted the air. Moose yelped and ran smack into Celie. Celie tumbled to the grass as she and Moose tangled together, trying to get to their feet. July reached to pull Celie free of the terrified dog. Celie clutched July in a death grip and yanked, struggling to get up. Instead, July toppled into the pile. Moose yapped with complaint, placed one paw on Celie's nose, and wedged his other paw in July's armpit; he then exploded with a massive surge of energy and tore out of sight, baying like a train racing downhill into the distance. July and Celie let themselves sprawl out on the ground.

"Stay planted right there," a familiar voice thundered from close by.

The girls froze. The Dragon was crossing the dry grass toward them with a scatter gun cradled in her arms.

"Keep your mouth closed. She's got a shotgun!" July gasped.

"Oh … oh … oh …" Celie was starting to panic.

"Celie, get quiet. Stick your hand in your mouth or something. She's got a shotgun," July hissed.

"Oh … oh … oh …" Celie continued.

"Celie, hand in the mouth!" July ordered. Celie did as July told her.

The Dragon stopped and looked down on them. "You again? I should have guessed it would be you, Miss Calendar and Miss Calendar."

Neither of the girls uttered a word. July thought this might be worse than The Dragon with an axe.

Mrs. Drunyon continued, "Was that bungling dog yours?"

July swallowed. "No, ma'am."

"Then does it belong to Mr. Calendar? And if so, where is Mr. Calendar? He wouldn't be snooping on my property again, would he?" The Dragon swerved her head about, intently searching her property.

July tried to get her attention. "Moose isn't Levi's dog either." July knew she had to do something before The Dragon went to the shed. She had to give the boys time to get out of there or hide. She had to lie, and she wasn't feeling so good about it. But if The Dragon found Levi and Franklin while she had a shotgun, those boys would be goners. July struggled to her feet. "Mrs. Drunyon, we saw Moose in your yard, and we were trying to get him out before you came home. We remembered from school today that you didn't much like dogs, so we were trying to help you," July insisted.

The Dragon whipped her head to Celie and placed her cool eyes on the girl. "Is that the truth, Miss Calendar?"

Celie stood but couldn't get her voice to make a sound, so she nodded her head to agree with the lie.

The Dragon sniffed. "Maybe ... maybe not ... but I think I'll take a gander in the shed and check Maxworth's Model-T. That's where I found all of you the last time you trespassed."

A loud crack followed by a crash came from the far side of the shed. The Dragon turned and glared at the girls. "No one else with you?" she demanded.

Celie slid behind July, and in terror wrapped her arms around her cousin. July knew what the sound had to be. The boys were making their escape. They must have gone up the ladder into the loft and climbed out the window. But that crash meant someone had fallen from the Cedar tree, or maybe a branch had broken.

The Dragon turned and pointed the shotgun toward the sound of the crash. "Right there. I don't want either of you two Calendars to move from that spot," she ordered. Then she started toward the side of the shed where the noise had come from.

"Wait," said July.

The Dragon turned her head.

"Mrs. Drunyon, that is where Moose ran to." July lied again, hoping to keep Mrs. Drunyon away from the boys, or at least give them time to escape.

"Moose?" The Dragon asked, her eyes narrowing into slits.

"Moose, the dog you shot, Mrs. Drunyon," July said. She was shaking all over.

"I'll see about that. If it is that mutt, I may finish him off." Mrs. Drunyon cocked the shotgun and marched toward the other side of the shed.

Celie tugged at July's dress. "What are we going to do? We can't let her kill Moose."

"We're going to run!" And run they did. They ran up the block and around the corner to get out of sight as fast as they could, almost smacking into Levi and Franklin who were running from the other direction. All four skidded to a stop, gasping for breath.

Levi choked out the words, "Follow me!" They stampeded again, not stopping until Levi dove under the big Cedar row between his house and Grams and Gramps's house. Levi scrambled into their hideout. They all followed. No one uttered a word. They could barely breathe, much less talk.

Celie was the first to speak. "But Prissy said the doctors at Larned State Hospital dismissed her because she was well."

July answered, "Then I guess Prissy doesn't know everything."

While Celie and July were discussing Prissy, Levi and Franklin were heehawing for some unknown reason.

Celie suddenly belted out, "Quit it, Levi. I have had it, and I'm going to tell Mama."

"What? What did I do?" Levi asked innocently.

"You know." Celie tried to scoot farther away from her brother, but there was no more room in the hideout.

"No, I don't know what you mean," Levi snickered.

"Levi, you know I don't like that. I don't like it when you put spit on your fingers and slide them down my face," Celie complained.

Levi chuckled.

"It isn't funny," Celie sobbed.

"Yes, it is. Look, Celie." Levi's smirking face was looking down. Franklin and July had joined the laughter.

Celie followed Levi's gaze. Moose! The hound squeezed his head between Celie and Levi and again swiped his tongue alongside her cheek. "Moose," Celie groaned. "I see The Dragon missed. I don't know if I'm sorry or not. If I wasn't so scared of her, I'd drag you over to her house and give you to her right now."

"No you wouldn't," Levi said. "You're a scaredy-cat girl."

"Of The Dragon? You better believe I am," Celie admitted gladly.

Franklin grinned. "But July isn't a scaredy-cat girl. July saved our bacon today," Franklin declared with admiration.

July felt a blush wash over her face.

"Eww." Levi gagged. "July is a girl, Franklin."

"I know," Franklin beamed.

"Hey," Celie interrupted. "Moose's ear is bleeding."

"What? The Dragon shot Moose?" Franklin urgently scooted over to his dog.

Celie tried to calm him. "Just his ear. The Dragon only pierced Moose's ear." Celie patted the dog. "Poor, poor Moose. Maybe we can put an earring in your ear." Celie giggled and hugged the poor dog.

11

The Paper Airplane

IT had been over a week since the haunted shed incident. The Dragon had said nothing, but she had changed the seating arrangements at school. Now, July, Celie, Franklin, and Levi, were front and center. As Mrs. Drunyon lectured, she would pace back and forth before them with a heavy stick. Every now and again she would whack it on one of their desks, causing the whole class to jump. At least with this seating arrangement they could watch out for each other.

The rest of the students wanted no part of the trouble July, Celie, Levi, and Franklin seemed to be in, so they hardly talked to them. They were the last chosen on any team, and school wasn't nearly as fun for anyone. Prissy seethed every time she let her eyes stray to the four front-row students. July knew she watched them. She could feel Prissy's glare burning into her back.

Moose's ear was healing nicely. Franklin liked Celie's idea of an earring, so he rummaged through his treasure collection. He found a pair of wire-rim glasses that were broken in half, so he twisted off the ear stem and nose piece and filed down any rough edges that remained. The tiny screw fixed to hold the glass lens in place was still there, so Franklin unscrewed it and pulled the wire rim apart. He slipped it into Moose's ear and tightened the screw securely back in place. Franklin was proud of his hound, and he thought the earring gave Moose class.

Moose still followed his master to school each day, but the hound would scoot under the porch the minute Mrs. Drunyon showed up on the scene. Moose would lay in the shade and wait for Franklin to get out of school.

One morning, Mrs. Drunyon stopped her pacing and stood in front of July's desk. She rapped the edge of it before she spoke. "I pray all of my students remembered to put their homework in the homework basket upon arrival this morning. I will be checking the papers while I have my lunch. You are all dismissed for one hour." Before anyone moved she added, "Please do not bother me. You know the rules. I expect you to abide by them, even though I am not outside with you. You older students are in charge of the younger ones."

When she finished, no one jumped and ran for the doorway. The students wanted to, but they were afraid of Mrs. Drunyon. Her dismissal was very orderly. The students in the back row stood together, picked up their lunch and walked out the door. Then the next to the back row and so on. The front row, July's row, was always last.

Outside, the haunted-shed group sat together beside the porch so Moose could edge his nose from beneath the floorboards and catch little bites of lunch that the group tossed to him. No one else joined them. No one wanted to be guilty by association.

Celie swallowed a hunk of her peanut butter and jelly sandwich. "I think we need to find some grownup to tell about Mrs. Drunyon still being crazy. Larned State Hospital must have made a mistake in dismissing her, and she sure shouldn't be our teacher," Celie whined.

Levi stopped chewing and asked, "Celie, how are you going to do that without telling them that we were on The Dragon's property, and without permission?"

"You mean trespassing?" July asked.

"Where were you trespassing?" Prissy had snuck up behind the group. She wedged her shoe between Franklin and July. Both moved away from her foot, so Prissy dropped into the open space. It was tight, but she didn't mind.

Not one of the group answered. Prissy didn't care. She opened her lunch but then stopped mid-air. "Franklin, what is wrong with your dog's ear?"

Franklin stared silently at Prissy. Levi cleared his throat and dove in with the answer. "Franklin pierced it. He thought it might start a new fashion ... for dogs."

Franklin nodded. "Yep. It looks pretty good."

Prissy gazed at Franklin, and he started to sweat. "Did you steal the earring from your mother?" she asked. "It's a rather plain thing and a bit beat up. I could probably get one from my mother with a diamond in it. Mother would let me have it for sure since she lost the other one."

"You would put a real diamond on a dog's ear?" July questioned.

Prissy fluttered her lashes at Franklin. "For Franklin I would."

Franklin jammed a whole boiled egg in his mouth so he wouldn't have to talk.

Prissy continued, "So what did you think of our weekend homework assignment?"

Levi blurted out, "Twenty-five long division problems? It took me two solid hours on Saturday. I sure wish Miss Smith was back. She never gave weekend homework."

"Mrs. Harms." Prissy corrected then touched the knee of Franklin's striped overalls. "You probably got it done in no time at all. You are so good in arithmetic."

Franklin shrugged and tried to scoot away.

Prissy smiled. "July and Celie, did you get your homework done?"

July nodded. She couldn't figure Prissy out. *Why did she want to know? Was it any of her business?* she wondered.

Celie answered, "You better believe I did my homework. If you don't do your work, you have double to do the next time, and Mrs. Drunyon said she might even make you stay after school with her to do it."

Prissy raised her eyebrows. "Mrs. Drunyon? I thought this little group," she twirled her finger in a circle, "called her *The Dragon*."

Celie slapped her hand over her mouth. Levi and Franklin stared at Prissy. July watched the girl. Prissy was up to something.

Prissy stood. "I'm going to go check on the other kids. Franklin, if you would like, you can come with me."

Franklin was at a loss for words. Finally, he stuttered, "N…n… naw, I got to stay close to Moose."

Prissy nodded. "If you want that earring, Franklin, let me know." As she turned, she shifted her eyes toward July and smirked.

Levi watched her walk away. "What was that all about?" he asked.

"I don't know," July answered. "But she has something planned, and I'll bet it's not good."

Celie giggled. "Prissy sure does like Franklin. She likes Franklin enough to give Moose a diamond earring for his shotgun-pierced ear."

"I like the gold ring just like it is, bent up and all." Franklin frowned.

Mrs. Drunyon blew her whistle which meant the only free time of their school day was over. The kids lined up and filed in.

That afternoon, Mrs. Drunyon paced in front of the first row several times before she stopped. She crossed her arms and tapped July's desk with her stick.

July didn't move.

"Miss Calendar, do you have your homework?"

"Yes, ma'am, Mrs. Drunyon," July said.

"Then you had best turn it in," Mrs. Drunyon instructed.

July's head flew up. "I already did. I put it in the homework basket the minute we filed in to class this morning."

Mrs. Drunyon tucked in her chin, doubting July's answer. "I went through every paper in that basket, and yours was not there. I will run through them again, but I do warn you: If you have lied to me, things will not go well for you."

Mrs. Drunyon went to her desk and sat. The whole class watched in silence as their teacher went through the papers one by one. When she placed the last paper on the pile, she looked up and steadied her gaze on July. "There is no paper with your name, Miss Calendar. You will be staying after school today for an hour. If you do not finish in that time, you will be staying after school tomorrow, also. Is that understood?"

"Yes, ma'am, Mrs. Drunyon," July said. She hesitated before she raised her hand.

"Miss Calendar?" Mrs. Drunyon asked impatiently.

"May I look through my things? I know I did my homework," July insisted.

Mrs. Drunyon nodded reluctantly.

July rippled through her tablet. Slowly she thumbed through it again. Nothing. She could feel her heart pounding.

"No homework?" Mrs. Drunyon sneered.

July shook her head.

"Very well; after school, Miss Calendar. Let us get back to work. We have lost precious time as it is." She turned to the blackboard and began to write.

Celie reached over to comfort July. She whispered, "I saw you put it in the homework basket. What happened?"

July shrugged. "Prissy. That's what happened. I don't know how, but I feel it in my gut. It was Prissy. It had to be."

Celie agreed. "Remember how strange she was acting at lunch break? I'll bet you're right."

"I know I am." July sighed.

"My rule of no talking still stands, Calendar girls, so unless you would like to join your cousin in her special after school program, Celie, I suggest you be quiet." Mrs. Drunyon didn't even turn away from writing on the blackboard.

The quiet was so thick July could almost hear it. From somewhere over July's shoulder, a crinkled up paper airplane flew to the front of the classroom, hitting the side of the chalkboard.

The Dragon stopped writing, slowly pivoted, and glared at the class. "Who threw this?" she asked as she picked up the crashed airplane.

Prissy's hand shot up. "I'm not sure, but I think it came from July's direction," she offered smugly.

Mrs. Drunyon laid her chalk on the ledge, crossed to her chair and sat. She took the crinkled airplane and spread it out. "Miss Calendar, it appears you were correct. This is your homework miraculously piloted through the air, which is not acceptable. Next time, Miss Calendar, put it in the basket."

July leaned back and slid down in her chair with relief. She wasn't sure what exactly had happened, but she didn't care. Her homework was there, and she was glad. "Thank you, Lord." Her heart drummed.

As Mrs. Drunyon turned the paper over to place it in the homework basket, her face hardened and began to glow red hot. Her eyebrows shot to her hair line, and sparks jumped from her eyes. She stood so fast that her chair skidded behind her, hitting the wall. The chalk toppled to the floor and busted. The Dragon tramped over to July's desk and placed the paper in front of her. "Is this your idea of a good joke?"

July's gaze fell to the paper on her desk, and her stomach rolled. A picture of a scaly, fire-breathing dragon had been drawn on the back of her homework. Underneath was the caption: Mrs. Drunyon: The Dragon.

12

The Judas Kiss

MRS. Drunyon whisked the paper from July's desk and scolded, "We will talk about this after school today." She fished a key from beneath her blouse, unlocked the top drawer, and placed July's homework inside, slamming the drawer and locking it. When she turned back to the chalkboard, the students expected her to finish writing the interrupted lesson, but instead, she walked into the storage room behind the chalkboard and disappeared. The whole class could hear her rummaging around in the closet, but few dared to move or say a word.

Levi stretched his head around Franklin and grinned at July. "That must be The Dragon's den."

"Not funny, Levi." July clipped the words.

Franklin leaned closer to July. "Did you draw that dragon? It was evil looking, but it's still pretty good art work."

July shook her head. "There is no way I would draw that on the back of my homework."

Now even more curious, Franklin asked, "Then who did?"

July whispered, "It had to be Prissy."

Franklin nodded and wiggled about in his seat to look at Prissy. Levi, Celie, and July did the same. Since she was taller than most,

Prissy was in the very back row. Prissy had her jaw set and a weasel-like smile on her face. She unfolded a piece of paper and held it up so July could read it:

Told you I would take care of you!

July's blood turned cold. Prissy was getting even or 'taking care of' July, but there was nothing to get even for. July was only being a friend to Franklin, and there was nothing wrong with that. Besides, she was only ten, and she was pretty sure Grams and Gramps would lock her in her room for a few years if they thought she had a boyfriend. Anyway, she didn't even want a boyfriend. Something must be wrong with Prissy.

Dear Jesus, please help me because I don't know what to do, July prayed. She placed her hand over the place where she wore her mother's wedding ring and suddenly groaned. After her problems last year with Mrs. Drunyon over her mother's ring, July hadn't been wearing it to school since The Dragon took over. But yesterday was Sunday. July loved Sundays. She could fasten Mama's ring on the golden chain Aunt Sybil had given her without worrying about The Dragon taking it. However, today was Monday, and she still had it on. Maybe she could get it to Celie for safe keeping. Quickly she unclasped the chain and pulled the necklace away.

When the Dragon slammed the storeroom door shut, July shook. She let her hands drop to her sides, and with the tiniest clink, July heard Mama's ring fall to the wooden floor beside Franklin's shoe. Mrs. Drunyon was watching, so July didn't dare move. She couldn't let that woman see the ring. The Dragon would take it. That ring was all she had left from Mama. Her heart raced along with thoughts of how to retrieve Mama's ring without The Dragon seeing.

Franklin put his elbows on his desk and cupped his chin in his hands. Then he placed his foot on top of July's necklace and drug it toward him.

July blinked. Did Franklin know what he had done?

"Miss Calendar," Mrs. Drunyon called. She had a broken-backed chair in one hand and something that looked like a circus hat in the other.

"Yes, ma'am, Mrs. Drunyon," July answered.

"Up front please. Your seat will be in this corner for the rest of the day," Mrs. Drunyon ordered.

July stood and reached for her tablet and pencil.

"For more art work, Miss Calendar? I think not. You will receive a zero in our afternoon classes." The teacher set the broken chair in the corner facing away from the rest of the class.

July felt as if she were walking to the gallows. The quiet in the room was like a brick wall. She was on one side and everyone else on the other.

Prissy raised her hand.

"Yes, Miss Overton," Mrs. Drunyon said.

"I really hate to tattle, but I think I saw July drop a note to Franklin. It's under his foot," Prissy gloated.

July turned and stared at her enemy.

A ghastly look grew over Franklin's face as Mrs. Drunyon headed his way.

"Mr. Franklin, lift your shoe," Mrs. Drunyon ordered.

Franklin lifted the one closest to Levi. There was nothing there.

"Now the other shoe." The Dragon kept her beady eyes on the boy.

Franklin pulled his foot off the floor. There was no note, and there was no ring on a chain.

July trembled. What had happened to her Mama's ring? She had watched where it landed, and she had seen Franklin put his foot on top of it, but where was it now?

The Dragon sighed. "Stand up, Mr. Franklin. Do you have a note in one of those pockets?"

Franklin shook his head.

The Dragon crossed her arms and tapped the toe of her heavy shoe. "If only I could believe you, young man." She looked at Levi. "I do not believe I can trust you." Her eyes then roved over the class, stopping on six-year-old Henry Barns. "Mr. Barns, you have small hands. Come search Mr. Franklin's pockets."

Young Henry Barns was terrified of The Dragon. He shuffled forward with his hands in his pockets and stood shaking in front of his teacher.

"Mr. Barns, I want you to pull everything out of Mr. Franklin's pockets and put it on his desk," Mrs. Drunyon instructed.

Henry nodded and began. From the first pocket, Henry took three marbles, six pop bottle lids and a rusty screw. The next pocket held wadded paper which had been wrapped about his lunch and an old snuff can with homemade fishing hooks in it. From the bib pockets of Franklin's overalls Henry took a stubby pencil, a torn ticket to the movie theatre, one penny and a square of flour sack material spackled in pink flowers with the name JULY written on it.

Levi chuckled, and Franklin glowered at his friend.

One back pocket had a well-worn handkerchief which Henry dropped like it was on fire and gagged.

The class snickered.

"That will be enough." Mrs. Drunyon cleared her throat. "One more pockets, Mr. Barns."

July held her breath. If her Mama's ring was in one of Franklin's pocket, it had to be this one.

Henry reached into the last pocket and yanked out a piece of folded paper.

Before it even touched the top of Franklin's desk, Mrs. Drunyon had it in hand.

The class gasped, and Prissy smiled. "I told you he had a note."

Mrs. Drunyon unfolded the paper and studied it. "What is this, Mr. Franklin?"

"It's a drawing of a skunk trap. We've been having skunk trouble at home, and I thought this might work." Franklin grinned.

"So it might." Mrs. Drunyon folded the blueprint and handed it back to Franklin. "Put the rest of your things back in your pockets, and don't let me catch you playing with any of that junk in my class." She looked at Henry. "Mr. Barns, you may go back to your seat."

The little boy nearly ran. Prissy crossed her arms and scooted down to pout in her seat. Mrs. Drunyon took the moment to lecture the class about writing notes. If any notes were found, they would be pinned to the wall and left for all to read.

But where was the ring? July wondered.

July sat in the broken chair with her face to the wall. Mrs. Drunyon had smashed the dunce hat atop her head. She would be getting a zero in arithmetic and penmanship this afternoon, but she didn't care. She wished she never had to see Prissy or The Dragon again. July wished she could go back to before her mother died and her world had been ripped apart. She stopped. The only good thing in that world had been Mama and her love. Everything else was cold and ugly. It was a world where they struggled for food, clothes and shelter. A world full of hurt, sickness and danger.

No. She did not want to go back to that world. Now she had a real home with her own room and family who loved her. Even Levi, who got her into plenty of trouble, would stand up for her and protect her. Then there was Franklin. He was a true friend, and he came with Moose. July smiled as the picture of Moose with his pierced ear crossed her mind.

The afternoon stretched on. She could hear pencils scratching on papers and papers rustling. The clock on the wall above her was ticking out her sentence. She not only heard but felt the steady rhythm of Mrs. Drunyon making rounds about the room on guard patrol.

Mrs. Drunyon stopped in front of the class and clapped her hands. "Put your work away. Be sure you have your homework assignment and your lunch things, and then we will be dismissed."

Prissy raised her hand.

"Miss Overton," Mrs. Drunyon called.

"Mrs. Drunyon, would you like me to erase the blackboard before I leave? My mother told me I could do that if you wished," Prissy said.

"Thank you, Prissy. That would be nice." Mrs. Drunyon gave one of her few smiles. It wasn't a big smile, and it didn't last long.

As the students filed out the door, Prissy went to the blackboard. She took the eraser and started swiping the section of the board closest to July. "I know you passed something to Franklin. I saw you do it. Was it a love note?" she demanded.

"No, Prissy, but if it was, it would be none of your business," July said.

Prissy's eyes blazed. "It was a love note, wasn't it?" Prissy didn't wait for July to answer. "I already warned you to stay away from Franklin. He's mine."

"Franklin doesn't want to be yours," July told her.

"Franklin doesn't know what he wants. If you stay away from him, he can like me," Prissy wailed.

"It doesn't work that way. Try being nice. If you would be nice to Franklin, he might like you," July said.

"But you are in my way. All Franklin notices is you," Prissy whined.

"Prissy, maybe I can help you learn how to be nice." July felt a warmth spread through her. This must be what Gramps had meant by turning the other cheek.

"How could you help?" Prissy asked suspiciously.

"It isn't hard. Say nice things, and do nice things. Don't always threaten to beat up people, and try smiling," July listed a few.

Prissy looked at July with indecision. Finally, she leaned over and kissed July on the cheek. "Thank you, July. Maybe we could be friends."

July felt a cold shiver crawl up her spine. Was it this easy? Gramps had said turning the other cheek could work miracles, but she thought it would take more than giving Prissy a couple of ideas. July nodded. Truly this would be a miracle.

Prissy erased the rest of the blackboard. Mrs. Drunyon walked into the room, thanked, and excused Prissy.

When Prissy's footsteps faded away, Mrs. Drunyon prepared to chastise July. She sat at her desk and told the girl to come stand in front of her. As July stood, a folded piece of paper fluttered to the floor. July stood still. Both sets of eyes landed on the paper. In the momentary silence that followed, the clock ticked, marking time passing. Finally, Mrs. Drunyon spoke. "Bring the note here, Miss Calendar."

July picked up the paper and took it to Mrs. Drunyon's desk. She didn't have to read it. She knew it would be incriminating evidence. That kiss Prissy had given her was to mask Prissy planting the note. So much for miracles.

Mrs. Drunyon unfolded the note and read:

Dear Franklin,

I like you, too, I would be glad to meet you behind the Cottonwood tree after school.

Love and kisses,

July

P.S.   J. C.

+

F. F.

"Miss Calendar, do you have an explanation?" asked Mrs. Drunyon.

July was defeated. "No, ma'am, Mrs. Drunyon. I just know I didn't write that note."

"July," said Mrs. Drunyon.

Stunned, July stared at her teacher. She had always called her "Miss Calendar," even before she had been her teacher.

Mrs. Drunyon continued, "I believe you."

July gaped in awe at The Dragon. "You do?"

"I do."

"Why?" July asked.

"I was standing in the door when Prissy kissed you. I watched her drop this folded paper behind you so when you stood, it would be found," Mrs. Drunyon explained.

Mrs. Drunyon stood and paced around her desk. She seemed to be thinking, and July was still overwhelmed. The Dragon stopped, picked up her stick she used to tap on students' desks, and whacked it in the palm of her hand a few times. She reached over with the stick and placed it on July's chest where her Mama's ring usually hung. "You still have something that is mine, and I want it."

Fear swelled through July's body. She backed away from The Dragon and rubbed her chest where the stick had been. "Mrs. Drunyon, I don't have it."

"Then where is it?" The Dragon eyes glowed as she leaned in closer.

July shrugged. "I don't know." July felt tears building up to a storm, and a knot was growing in the pit of her stomach. She shuddered. She didn't have to lie to The Dragon. She really didn't know where her Mama's ring was.

The Ring

BEFORE the cloud burst of tears broke, July rushed out of the schoolhouse, across the porch, and down the steps. July only glanced back once to see The Dragon on the porch steps with her stick raised in the air, shouting. July didn't know what she was saying, and she didn't care. She didn't stop running until she scrambled beneath the big Cedar in her tree row, leaned against the trunk and sobbed. Did God understand how mean her enemies were? She was under the master rule of The Dragon, who July felt wanted to chew her up and spit her out. She didn't care if she never saw The Dragon again. In fact, she wished she didn't have to. However, she had to go back to school tomorrow. Waiting for her would be The Dragon ... and Prissy, or Judas, as July would think of her now.

The branches parted, and Celie ducked in. "I'm sorry, July. I waited outside the school window for you in case I needed to run for help. I saw what Prissy did, but at least The Dragon saw her do it, too. Prissy finally got caught in her own trap, and I'm glad." Celie added, "But what you said to Prissy was so nice. I think that is why God let her get caught. It protected you from The Dragon, and maybe now that awful woman will see Prissy's true colors."

July didn't say a word. *Had turning the other cheek worked in what Gramps called 'mysterious ways'?* She didn't get in trouble, and who knows how much trouble Prissy might be in when she comes to school tomorrow. July didn't think The Dragon would let it pass ... not while she was in charge.

Celie reached over and pressed her hand on July's hand. "I am really sorry about your mama's ring. I saw it fall, but I don't know what happened to it."

July wiped her wet cheeks with her hands.

Celie asked, "What did happen?"

July leaned her head back against the tree trunk and looked to the top of its branches. "I don't know. I forgot to take my necklace off before I went to school. I like to sleep with it because it makes me feel close to Mama, but I take it off for school so The Dragon can't see it. Today I forgot, and I was afraid The Dragon would take it when I stayed after school. While Mrs. Drunyon was in the closet, I took it off. I was going to sneak it to you so you could get it home for me. But when she stormed out of the closet, it scared me so much I dropped it. Franklin covered it with his foot, and I don't know if he knew it was there or not." July pulled her gaze from the top of the tree and looked at Celie. "My mama's ring is gone, Celie. I don't know what happened to it, but I know it's gone." July was crying again.

Celie caressed July's hand. "Maybe it's still on the floor somewhere around Franklin's desk. We can go back and check. I saw The Dragon lock the door before she left, so we'll have to go through the window."

"Did The Dragon sweep before she went home? If she did, it's gone," July moaned.

"No. She didn't have time to sweep. She barely had time to get her things. She looked like she was on a mission. So there's a chance your mama's ring is still there," Celie said enthusiastically.

"Coming in," warned Levi as he swished through the Cedar branches followed by Franklin. Moose belly crawled beneath the tree, sniffed July, then whined and snuggled against her leg. He seemed to know she felt badly, and he was trying to comfort her by pounding his tail, which kept slapping Celie.

With both hands Celie took his tail and held it tight. "Don't wag your mangy tail on me, Moose Mange." Moose slid his tongue across Celie's arm. She wiped it off alongside her skirt. "Ugh, Moose Mange!"

Franklin laughed. "Celie, you are going to end up liking that hound."

"I am not. He stinks. Does he ever brush his teeth?" Celie groaned.

"He's a dog. When he gnaws on a bone, it cleans his teeth," Levi added.

"What would you know about it?" Celie chided.

Franklin grinned. "Levi's right, Celie."

Celie looked at the dog and shook her head. "That is disgusting. Don't ever lick me again, Moose Mange."

Everyone laughed but Celie.

When they had settled, Celie spoke, "We are going back to the school. July dropped her necklace somewhere around her desk, and we have to find it."

Levi sobered. "Your mama's ring? That necklace?"

July nodded. "I have to find it before The Dragon does. She wants it, and she will keep it."

"Yep," Levi agreed. "But The Dragon probably locked the school."

Celie nodded. "She did, but with your help, we can get through a window."

Levi looked grim. "I don't know. If we get caught, it will be breaking and entering, and that could mean reform school."

Celie gasped. "You didn't care about that when you and Franklin wanted to go in The Dragon's haunted shed."

"You can't call it breaking and entering if there is no door to break through. We just walked in." Levi planted a fake grin on his face.

"So it's 'walking and entering'? I 'spose you can go to reform school for that, too, Levi. You sure didn't have permission from The Dragon," Celie accused.

Franklin held up his hand. "Whoa, I might have something to say about this."

Celie narrowed her eyes. "Franklin D. Franklin, I'm surprised at you. I knew Levi would be afraid to crawl through the schoolhouse window unless it was his idea, but I thought for sure you wouldn't be afraid," she challenged.

Franklin chuckled. "Quit jumping at skeeters." Shyly he glanced at July then to the ground before he continued. "I would do anything for July."

"Then why not crawl through a window?" Celie demanded.

"Because we don't need to," Franklin said.

"And why not?" Celie argued.

Franklin stuck his hand in the hide-away pocket of his overalls and pulled out a gold chain with a ring dangling from it. Franklin shrugged. "I was sweating for sure during The Dragon's search, and hoping and praying. But unless you wear overalls, you don't know about this here little hide-away pocket." Franklin patted his pocket. "Henry don't wear overalls, and I guess neither does The Dragon." Franklin placed the priceless treasure in the palm of July's hand.

July cradled it. "Thank you, Franklin. I didn't even know if you knew I dropped it."

"I don't miss much in The Dragon's class. You have to keep on your toes. It doesn't seem she likes kids over much, but I think she has it out for you especially," Franklin told her.

"You can say that for sure," Levi chimed in, relieved there would be no breaking and entering today.

July nodded. "And it's not just Mrs. Drunyon. Prissy doesn't like me either." She hesitated to explain the reason why.

But Celie didn't. "Prissy doesn't like you because she is too busy liking Franklin."

No one disagreed. They all sat quietly under the shade of the Cedar. It was Levi who broke the silence. "We have to put up with The Dragon clear until Christmas break. I don't know if I can handle it. She gives weekend homework, and school isn't any fun at all now that Miss Smith is gone," Levi bemoaned.

Celie, not correcting Levi with Miss Smith's married name, gave a knowing smile to July. Levi had had a crush on Mrs. Harms before she got married. Levi drudged on, "Now school is probably a lot like reform school except we get to go home at night." He turned to Franklin. "You're lucky. I'll bet you could quit school."

Franklin thumped a Cedar sprig. "Pa wouldn't care, but Ma would put her foot down. There is no way she'll let me quit. She says an education is important."

It was quiet until Franklin spoke again. "I don't have an idea about The Dragon, but maybe I can get Prissy off your case."

"How?" July asked.

Franklin took a deep breath and slowly blew it out before he stated flatly, "I could like Prissy."

"You could do that?" Celie looked doubtful.

"You would do that?" Levi frowned.

Franklin shrugged. "If I have to … for July."

"No," July said. "Gramps told me to turn the other cheek. He said it would work. He didn't say how long it would take, but Gramps told me it's in the Good Book."

"How does that work?" Franklin asked.

Levi responded, "I know how it works. It doesn't."

"That's because you have to be nice to your enemy. Levi doesn't have the guts to be nice to his enemy," Celie said.

"If you hadn't been the enemy, Celie, I could a done it," Levi growled.

July and Franklin laughed.

"Franklin," July started, "it is something Gramps gave me to do, so it is my job. And I have seen it work twice now. Oh, it isn't anything big, but it kept me out of trouble. Today after school, Prissy planted a love note on me which she had written. She signed my name, and I thought it was going to get me in a big mess with The Dragon. Guess what? Mrs. Drunyon saw Prissy plant the note. I thought I would fall over when The Dragon said, 'I believe you, July.'"

"Are you sure you don't want me to act like I got a crush on Prissy?" Franklin asked.

"I'm sure." July nodded. "But maybe we could all be nice to Prissy. There might be so many turning cheeks that Prissy won't know who to be mean to."

"I can do that," Franklin said.

"Me, too," Celie agreed.

Levi was silent but finally conceded. "Prissy? It will be like eating raw liver, but I'll try."

"July?" From beyond the trees they all heard Gramps call her name.

July scooted from their secret hiding place. Gramps was waiting on the porch for her. "July, we have a guest, and he needs you to answer a few questions." Gramps held the screen door for his granddaughter.

July stepped in the kitchen, and sitting at the table was her lawyer friend. A smile lit July's face. "Good afternoon, Mr. Sam Bryan."

"A good afternoon to you, too, Miss June July Calendar." Then Mr. Bryan pulled out a chair beside him for her to sit in. "How are you doing in our Plevna school?"

July stared at him. She knew he was a lawyer and a smart man. She wondered if he knew about Mrs. Drunyon being their teacher.

She tipped her head to the side. "School is fine," she answered cautiously.

Mr. Bryan cleared his throat. "July, I know the lady who brought you here from the orphanage, Mrs. Drunyon, is your temporary teacher."

July slapped her mama's ring down in the middle of the table. "Then you may as well know, I won't be wearing this to school again. I am going to search out a hiding place for it so no one will ever find it."

"July, has Mrs. Drunyon tried to take your ring?" the lawyer asked.

July studied him. "Yes and no. I think she kept me after school today to try to take it."

"But she didn't?"

"No, sir. That is because she couldn't. I didn't have it, and I ran away from her," July answered proudly.

Across the table, Grams's eyes were flooding. Gramps pulled out a chair and sat.

Mr. Bryan continued, "I need to ask some questions, July. Do you remember anything about your father?"

July looked to the ceiling. "I remember he was tall and had big hands, but I was only about three. Maybe he was tall and had big hands because mine were little."

Mr. Bryan chuckled. "That very well could be, July. I want you to think hard about these questions. Did your mother have a box of important papers? Did she have a pocketbook to keep things she needed safe? Did your mother ever call your father by his name?"

July rested her chin in her hands and thought about each question before answering, "We lived in the alleys toward the end, and there wasn't any box. She did have a pocketbook, but I don't know what she kept in it. Besides, this big guy we called Brutus snatched it a couple of months before Mama died. We tried to stay away from Brutus, but he found our alley." July struggled to remember. "There might have been something important in her pocketbook because Mama cried. I remember she said something like, 'My home. My mama. My daddy. Everything is gone. Gone.' She kept crying and saying, 'Gone.' I didn't know what to do. I asked her if she wanted me to follow him and try to get it back, but she latched ahold of my hand and wouldn't let me go. By then Brutus was long gone, so I sat on the ground and rocked her until she went to sleep."

Grams was dabbing flowing tears with her handkerchief, and Gramps wasn't far from it. In the stillness Mr. Bryan asked, "Your father's name?"

July thought, but finally shook her head. "I can't remember anything."

"That is fine, July. Would you mind if I took a closer look at your mother's ring?" Mr. Bryan asked carefully.

"Why?" July began to panic.

"I am not taking it. I would just like a better look," the lawyer reassured the little girl.

July nodded.

Mr. Bryan gently picked up the ring. He rolled it in the light from the window. "Have you ever thought about getting this appraised?"

"What does that mean?" July asked.

Mr. Bryan smiled. "That is when you take it to a professional jeweler, and they tell you how much it's worth."

"I don't reckon it's valuable, knowing June. If it was, why didn't she sell it for the money?" asked Gramps.

"I don't know," Mr. Bryan said.

"Mr. Bryan, it's worth a whole lot to me, even if it isn't worth anything at all," July told him.

"Well look at this." the lawyer tipped the ring in the light. "There are some initials on the inside of the band. I'm not sure I can make them out. Hmm ... one looks to be a 'D.'"

SANDRA WAGGONER

July cringed. *Mrs. Drunyon's name started with a 'D.' She claimed it was hers and that I had stolen it. No, it couldn't be. Mama's name was May June Calendar. None of those names started with a 'D!'*

14

The Visit with Mr. Bryan

JULY stared at the ring. Defiantly she lifted her head and looked at those around the table. Grams's face was frozen in shock. Gramps looked a bit sick at his stomach. The lawyer was still studying the ring.

"July, did you ever notice the initials before?" Mr. Bryan asked.

"No. I never even looked at the inside of the ring, but one thing I know, I didn't steal it. My mama gave it to me when she was dying." July was rigid. If she gave an inch, she felt she would fall apart.

"I believe you. There is no question in my mind that your mother gave this ring to you." Mr. Bryan took his little finger and rubbed the inside of the ring.

July relaxed a bit.

Mr. Bryan continued his questioning. "July, maybe your father's name started with a 'D.' Can you try to remember your mother calling him by his name?"

"I can't promise, but I'll try, if you think it will help," July spoke quietly.

"It might help. Did your mama ever say where she and your father got the ring? These are tight times. Maybe your father bought it in a pawn shop, or he could have traded with someone for the ring," the lawyer continued fishing.

July was at a loss. "I don't know. I was little the last time I saw my dad. When he didn't come back, after a while Mama quit talking about him." She paused. "Wait ... "

No one said a word to interrupt her thoughts. July looked at an empty space on the wall while she went back in time to the alleys which had been home. She talked slowly as memories flooded her mind. "When Mama took her ring off and handed it to me, she said something like, 'July, this is the most valuable thing I have.' Then she told me to hold on to it because it was a key. I didn't understand what she meant, and I tried to ask. Mama started coughing and choking, and I forgot about the key part until now. I already knew her ring was the most valuable thing she had because she didn't have anything else. And I knew I would keep it forever because it was Mama's ring."

Gramps put his arm around Grams to hold her close and to steady her shaking body.

Mr. Bryan spoke softly. "July, that is good. Now, I want you to take your mother's ring and put it in a special place. I also want you to continue to think about things your mother might have told you. They could be important clues. Also, I would suggest you do not wear your lovely necklace with your mother's ring to school again."

July's heart pounded as she asked, "Is Mrs. Drunyon trying to get my mama's ring?"

"Yes, she would like it, but she would have to prove it was her ring first. It would be better if you keep the ring at home," Mr. Bryan encouraged. "You know, they always say possession is nine-tenths of the law."

July gave one solid nod. "Thank you, Mr. Bryan, for believing that I didn't steal this." July spit in her hand, swiped it down the side of her dress and held it out for him to shake.

Grams was horrified. "July!" The lawyer winked at Grams and shook hands with the little girl.

Gramps was torn when he looked at July. "Honey, go on upstairs. Put your mama's ring in a safe place."

July paused. She knew they wanted to get her out of the kitchen because they were going to talk about things they didn't think she should hear. "Go on, July." Gramps waved toward the stairs.

July left the kitchen but stopped around the corner and sat on the step. She wanted to know what they were going to talk about. She had a right to know. After all, they were going to talk about her. Without even getting up, Gramps called, "July, on upstairs."

July sighed. *How did he know? Maybe he knew things because he was old. Maybe it was because he knew God. Maybe he listened for a secret sound from the step.*

July tromped on up the stairs, making as much noise as possible. She crossed to her closet and opened the door then shut it. She didn't slam it like she wished she could, but she shut it loud enough so Gramps would know she was in her room. She counted to fifty then stealthily eased her shoes off and tiptoed back down the stairs. She stopped right before the turn in the staircase and held her breath, waiting to see if she had been heard.

Gramps was talking. "Sam, has Mrs. Drunyon talked to you?"

Sam took a deep breath before admitting. "She did come to the office, Ezra. She asked me to take her case, but I told her I would have a conflict of interest. However, Mrs. Drunyon wanted me to know what I was getting into. She told me about the initials on the inside of the band."

July heard Gramps drumming his fingers on the table top like he always did when he was studying a matter, but Grams was the one who asked the question. "Sam, do you think July stole the ring?"

"No. Twice now July has told me the exact same story about how she came by the ring. I believe her. I really believe that little girl's mama gave it to her. I don't think she could make up those feelings.

And furthermore, I believe July will protect her mama's ring to the death. It's her link to her mother," Sam explained.

Grams asked quietly, "Do you think the ring belongs to Mrs. Drunyon?"

It was a moment before the lawyer answered. "I don't know, May. Mrs. Drunyon is aware of details about the ring July didn't even notice. How would she know those particulars if she had never had the ring? If the case does go to court, the question needing answered will be, 'How did July get the ring?'"

"What we need to know, Sam, is if the court were to find that the ring does belong to Mrs. Drunyon, can July be sent to reform school for theft?" asked Gramps.

"Well," Sam hesitated. "There is always that possibility. Usually I would say, 'No,' but with July's background and Mrs. Drunyon's accusations, July already has two strikes against her."

"Oh, Ezra," Grams moaned.

"The good Lord will see us through this, May." Gramps comforted her before he asked, "More coffee, Sam?"

July heard Gramps skid the chair over the floorboards and walk to the stove. July held her breath and hoped her pounding heart couldn't be heard. She listened as Gramps poured coffee, but she didn't relax until she heard his chair slide beneath the table again.

Mr. Bryan continued, "Have the two of you thought about adopting July?"

"Why?" Grams and Gramps responded at the same time.

"Legally it would give you better grounds on which to protect your granddaughter," the lawyer said.

Grams's voice was shaking. "Protect her? From what?"

Mr. Bryan took a moment before he answered. "I think it would shield her from reform school."

July could feel Gramps lean in closer to the lawyer. "There's more, isn't there?"

"Yes." Sam responded reluctantly. "Mrs. Drunyon assured me she would be getting a lawyer, and Mrs. Drunyon is not the only one who has been in my office with questions concerning July."

Both Gramps and Grams asked, "Who?"

"That I am not at liberty to answer. Without a doubt, I have said more than I should, but I knew you needed to be warned. I knew, too, you would want to pray," Sam replied.

A long, thoughtful moment passed before Grams almost whispered, "Sam, we don't have the money to adopt July."

Gramps's voice was gravelly but determined. "We have this place, May. If need be, we could sell it. It's only a house. We will do whatever must be done to save July. She's been through more in her ten years than most go through in a lifetime. It would tear her up something awful if she was yanked away from the only home she has ever had. We will fight for our granddaughter. We will fight to keep her."

The lawyer and friend stood to take his leave. "If there is anything I can do, without compromising the case, let me know. I will be more than happy to help."

"Thank you, Sam. You've been a good friend," Gramps told him.

When the screen door slammed, July heard Grams sobbing. She knew Gramps had taken her in his arms. "God will take us through."

Grams choked, "I cannot lose her, too. It was hard enough to have June torn from my life. I don't think I could handle having July yanked out of it now."

"Honey, we are going to pray. God is our Lord. He made the sun, the moon and the stars. He made the leviathan and the behemoth."

"And The Dragon," Grams interrupted.

Gramps chuckled. "Yes, May, he made The Dragon—probably so we would know we need God all that much more."

"In my heart I know you're right, Ezra," Grams agreed.

"And he made us. Without him was not anything made that was made. If our God can do those mighty works, is it not a simple task for God to keep a little girl in our arms?" Gramps preached.

Grams sniffed. "If you're going to preach at me, you'd best leave my kitchen."

Gramps chuckled. "Did it help?"

"Always."

"You going to cook up a storm now?" Gramps asked.

Grams laughed. "A hurricane. Cooking eases my soul from all my troubles. I can take a knife to the bacon, pound the bread, sear the onions, cut the potatoes and crack the eggs. If I picture the face of The Dragon on the meat, bread, onions, potatoes and eggs, it does wonders for me."

"Sunday morning, May, you'd best be at the altar," Gramps teased.

"Go on with you. While you pray, I'll cook." Grams ordered him out the door.

"Then I think I better to head to the church. I have some things I need to talk to the Lord about, but I'll be back before supper," Gramps promised.

July heard the screen door screech to a close.

"July," Grams called upstairs. "Would you come get the clothes basket and get the clothes off the line for me while I start supper?"

"Yes, Grams," July answered. "I'll be down in a minute." First there was something she would have to do. July lightly ran up the stairs, dropped to the side of her bed and prayed, "Dear Jesus, you have got to help me know what to do."

Outside, the September wind was lazy. It made the clothes on the line waltz to a slow, beautiful melody. The clothes smelled so fresh that July liked to bury her face in them. The whole time that she dropped clothes pins into the bag hanging on her side and flopped clothes into the basket, her mind was working on a plan. She sat on the porch to fold the clothes. By the time her task was done, so was her plan. "Grams," she called as she brought the basket inside the kitchen. "Can I go outside for a while?"

Grams was at the stove with her back to July. "Did you get the laundry folded?"

"Yes, ma'am," July assured her.

"Then I don't see why not. Don't go too far. Supper will be ready in about an hour." Grams turned and waved a wooden spoon.

July was out the door and off the porch. She knew where she was going, and there were two ways to get there. She would take the longer way because the other way went by the church where Gramps was, and she didn't want him to see her and ask questions. In five blocks, she was on Main Street. She walked down the street and right up to the office door of the Bryan Law Firm, mumbled a prayer, opened the door, and went inside.

The secretary looked up from her work. "May I help you?"

July nodded. "I would like to speak with Mr. Sam Bryan please."

The secretary smiled. "Mr. Bryan does not often have such young visitors. Are you here on business or pleasure?"

"Business. I need to hire a lawyer," July told her.

"Yes, ma'am. Whom may I tell him is here to see him?" the secretary asked pleasantly.

"June July Calendar, but everyone calls me July. And Mr. Bryan will know who I am for sure," July said.

The secretary grinned. "July, my name is Maple. Would you like to have a seat while I check to see if Mr. Bryan has an opening? Right now he is with a client."

July groaned, but she went to the stuffy couch and flopped down. "Boy, this is soft. I sure would have liked to have found something like this in an alley in Kansas City."

"Really? Plevna doesn't have too many alleys with couches." Maple laughed.

Waiting was not something July wanted to do, but she settled into the couch to do just that—wait. Supper was coming, and she knew better than to be late. She looked on the wall for a clock. Five-thirty. July wondered what time Mr. Bryan's office closed. Maple had started typing again. July snuggled back into the cushions. The door to the inner office opened, and Mr. Bryan walked out with an older lady who was wearing a rusty-colored hat with a spray of pheasant feathers. Bronze pearls swung from her neck and adorned her ears. "Thank you so much, Sam," she said as she reached up with her gloved hand on his shoulder, stood on her tiptoes and kissed his cheek.

"Any time, Tessie," Mr. Bryan replied. "I'm glad you're safely back from your six-month tour of Europe. I missed you. You come visit me anytime."

July was staring at the lady leaving Mr. Bryan's office when he spied the little girl. "In one day I am blessed with two such lovely ladies visiting me at my office. July, I would like you to meet my Aunt Tessie, but," he put his hand to the side of his mouth so his aunt wouldn't hear and whispered, "she doesn't like to be called Aunt. It makes her feel old. All the family calls her Tessie." He took his hand from his cheek and stated, "Tessie, this is my young friend, July."

July rose to shake her hand. Mr. Bryan intercepted her with a soft warning in her ear. "No spit, July. Tessie wouldn't understand."

"What wouldn't I understand, Sam? A spit shake? The only binding shake there is?" July watched Tessie's eyes twinkle. They were just like Mr. Bryan's twinkle. "However," his aunt continued, "at my age, it is better to spread as little germs as possible. I am delighted to meet you, young lady. July, is it?"

"Yes, ma'am," July responded.

"And a polite young lady. Do you have business here, my dear?" Tessie asked.

"I sure do. I am here to hire a lawyer," July told her.

Mr. Bryan stepped in. "Then you must come into my office, and July, if you don't mind, could Tessie join us? She always wanted to be a lawyer."

"You did?" July asked in awe.

"You bet your boots I did, but in my time, not too many women had the chance to be a lawyer. I have thought about going back to school to get my degree, but I've been twenty-nine and holding since women got the right to vote," Tessie explained.

"Jeepers, you are really pretty for an old lady," July whistled. Behind the secretary's desk, Maple gasped.

Mr. Bryan coughed to cover his humor, but his Aunt Tessie's laughter rippled through the room. "Youth is so carefree, and I love it. How about it, July? May I join you and Sam?"

July nodded. "Yes, ma'am."

"Tessie gave me my chance to be a lawyer. She helped me through school. I am trying to encourage her to go get that degree," Mr. Bryan said as he ushered them into his office and closed the door behind them.

"I was able to give a hand, thank the Lord, and my late husband, John Henry, God rest his soul. Both instructed me to help Sam," Tessie laughed.

When all were seated, the lawyer exclaimed, "July, let's talk business."

"Mr. Bryan, I listened to every word said at my house this afternoon, even though all of you wanted me gone." July thought it best to get the confession out of the way.

The lawyer raised his eyebrows. "Go on."

"I asked God about this. I know Grams and Gramps don't have the money to adopt me. I heard them say they would do anything, even sell their house, but I can't let them do that. I have lived in the streets, and it isn't any place for people as old as they are." July paused and stroked her tightly-closed fist with her other hand. "So, with this ring of my mama's, I want you to adopt me to them." She stretched out her hand holding her precious ring.

Mr. Bryan was stunned. "But July, that is all you have of your mother."

"But Mr. Bryan, their house is all they have." July was trembling as she laid the ring on his desk. "They would give all they have for me, so I guess I can give all I have for them. There has never been anyone on this whole earth, except Jesus, Gramps and Grams, who would do that for me."

Reverently Mr. Bryan spoke, "July, first we have to settle the ownership of the ring."

"I heard you say that possession is nine-tenths of the law. It's my ring, so I figure if we sell it before The Dragon, I mean, Mrs. Drunyon knows, she won't have anything to claim." July rested her case.

"Whatever I do, it will be legal. However, I would rather we wait until we find out if we need the ring. I will keep it safe for you; I promise." The lawyer picked up July's prized possession—not just a ring, but a piece of her heart.

"One other thing." July stayed his wrist. "You can't tell Grams and Gramps. Promise?"

Mr. Bryan stood and made an 'X' over his chest. "Cross my heart and hope to die."

"Thank you, Mr. Sam Bryan. I got to get home before Grams finds me gone." July spit, slid her hand over her dress, and shook with her lawyer friend.

Sam took her hand. "It has been nice doing business with you, June July Calendar."

Tessie watched the little girl walk to the outside door before asking, "So they call Mrs. Drunyon, 'The Dragon'?"

"Yes, they do," Mr. Bryan acknowledged.

Tessie wiped a tear from her rose-colored cheek. "I think I would slay a dragon for that child."

"We may have to, you and I." Sam Bryan was not an emotional man, but he gratefully took the extra handkerchief his aunt handed him.

The Confrontation

"**J**ULY?" Celie dashed from the end of the tree row. "You didn't forget and wear your mama's ring did you?"

July touched the empty spot. "Nothing there."

"Good. The Dragon knows where you keep it. I think she has x-ray eyes, and I bet they glow in the dark," Celie confided.

"Maybe, but I hope I never see her in the dark to find out. She's scary enough in broad daylight," July told her.

Celie squealed as Moose loped from behind and shoved his wet nose against the back of her knee. "Naughty Moose Mange. Stay away from me," she scolded.

Franklin laughed. "You know Moose can't help his nose being wet with snot. He's a dog."

"Snot?" Celie groaned as she wiped her hand across her knee and scraped it over the dry grass. Then she shook her finger at the dog. "Don't even think about touching me, Moose Mange."

Moose tipped his head and whined, his earring glimmering in the sunlight.

"You hurt his feelings, Celie." Franklin knelt on one knee beside his dog and scratched both of his floppy ears.

"Dogs don't have feelings," Celie told him.

"Want to bet he don't?" Levi offered eagerly. He was always ready for a bet.

"How can you prove something like that?" Celie asked.

"Franklin and I will show you," Levi promised. "If I'm wrong, I'll do your homework tonight. If you're wrong, you'll have to do mine. Deal?"

Celie debated for a moment before responding. "It would be a for sure bet. Dogs can't talk, and you can't prove it."

July shook her head. "I wouldn't, Celie. You know Levi and his bets."

Levi shrugged. "Suit yourself, but tonight's homework is your favorite: long, long, long division."

"I hate arithmetic," Celie groaned.

"Deal?" Levi stuck his hand out.

Celie nodded. "Deal." They slapped their hands together, and Celie felt she was looking at a sure win.

July shook her head. She remembered the bet she had made with Levi that he couldn't eat butter. That didn't turn out to be such a good deal.

July listened as Franklin, Levi, and Celie made their plans to prove or disprove that Moose had feelings.

At the school, they found a comfortable place in the grass facing the path to the school steps. When a student would walk by, Franklin would say, "How about it, Moose?" Moose would wag his tail and lop his tongue, pretty much showing he didn't have a clue as to what Franklin was asking.

Celie wagged her head from side to side the same as Moose wagged his tail. "I told you. Moose Mange doesn't know a thing."

Then Prissy skipped down the path. July knew what the boys were going to do. She warned, "You'd best leave Prissy alone. Remember, we are going to turn the other cheek and be nice to her."

Levi reasoned, "Just this once, July. Then we'll start being nice."

July shook her head. Levi would never learn. Prissy was within a couple of feet now. "How about it, Moose?" Franklin whispered. Moose rolled his dog lips back and growled.

Prissy jumped, turned, and scolded. "Franklin, you better be keeping that dog away from school. You know The Dragon doesn't like him."

"The Dragon?" Mrs. Drunyon had walked up behind Prissy. Prissy's mouth dropped open in horror.

Moose didn't wait for the "How about it, Moose?" He knew how he felt about The Dragon. The hound howled and plunged against Prissy, knocking her to the ground. Prissy was tangled in Moose's scrambling feet, and together they spun a complete circle, letting the dust fly. The terrified dog torpedoed through the children standing about, sending them scurrying. At the porch, he dropped to his belly and crawled to safety beneath the boards.

As the dust settled, Prissy gulped, her hands on the ground behind her propping her up. She nervously peeked above to find Mrs. Drunyon tapping her foot with her hands on her hips. Through clenched teeth, The Dragon hissed, "Prissy, did I hear correctly? The Dragon? You called me The Dragon?"

Prissy stuttered and lied, "It wasn't me." Tears welled up in her eyes.

"I know what I heard, young lady. I will see you in at my desk immediately." The Dragon whirled to slither away.

"Wait." July's heart beat against her lungs, making her struggle for each breath. Now was the time to turn the other cheek. "Ma'am, Mrs. Drunyon?"

The Dragon whipped around. "What?"

"It wasn't Prissy. I called you that. It was me."

The Dragon glared suspiciously at July. "You?"

July nodded.

"Get in the room now." The Dragon pointed toward the door.

Stumbling to his feet, Franklin, who would do anything to help July, stammered, "It wasn't July. It was me, Mrs. Drunyon. I called you The Dragon."

Celie scrambled to her feet and stammered, "Uh ... no! It was me. Uh ... it was me that called you ... umm ... The Dragon."

Levi threw his hands in the air, and from the ground he declared, "It was me that called you The Dragon, Mrs. Drunyon."

Prissy's cheeks glistened with tears.

The Dragon flashed her eyes from one child to the other and finally shouted, "All of you get in the schoolhouse. Now!"

Prissy didn't know if Mrs. Drunyon still meant for her to go, too. She squeaked the question out. "Do you still want me, also?"

The Dragon didn't even answer. She pointed a finger, and Prissy struggled to her feet and ran, following the others.

Mrs. Drunyon marched in behind the children and moved behind her desk. She studied each one. Prissy was so scared she grabbed July's hand. Celie already held July's other hand in a death grip. Levi and Franklin were being the perfect gentlemen. They were standing behind the girls.

In a low, seething voice Mrs. Drunyon began, "I will not tolerate this disrespect. Each of you will pen a note to your parents, or guardians as in July's case. I want the note to explain exactly what you have done. You will each be suspended for three days, and you will receive zeros for all work missed in that time. After school this evening, I want to meet with you and your parents so that we may discuss further action."

All five students stood petrified to their spots. Their hearts pounded in unison as they struggled for gulps of air. Mrs. Drunyon shooed them to their desks. "Go on. I intend to read each note before I excuse you, except July. I will talk to you now ... privately. Follow

me." The Dragon headed to the narrow storeroom behind her desk—
The Dragon's Den.

"Don't go, July," Celie whispered.

"I don't think I have a choice," July muttered.

Franklin stood cemented to his place. "Mrs. Drunyon, I'll come,
too. After all it was me that called you The Dragon."

Sparks seemed to fly from The Dragon's eyes as she whirled
about. "No, you won't. You will sit and write. This is between July and
myself." She flung open the door to the storeroom and waited until
July crossed the threshold before she shook her finger toward Franklin and the others. "Plaster yourselves in your seats," she ordered;
then she shut the door behind her.

She turned to July in the dim room. "You have something I
want. This would be a good time to give it to me."

July shook. She didn't know she could be so frightened. And
Celie was right. The Dragon's eyes did glow in the dark—almost.

The Dragon grabbed July's shoulders, and her claws dug in. "I
want my ring, you alley trash. You stole it, and I know you did. You
might be able to hide the fact from your grandparents, but I know
you for the thief you are. I want my ring."

"I ... I ... I ... don't have it." July stumbled through the words.
Tears were rolling down her cheeks. She didn't know when they
started, but they wouldn't stop.

"I know you have it. And since you have told all the students to
call me The Dragon, I will add the charge of defamation of character
to your charges of thievery and delinquency." Her claws dug deeper as
she shook the little girl. The Dragon then let go and swiftly whisked
her heavy shoe from her foot. She swung it back to strike July. July
gasped and kicked The Dragon as hard as she could. She ducked,
swerved around The Dragon, and escaped out of the supply closet.
July tore through the desks toward the outside door. The Dragon was
hot on her heels, the clunky shoe raised high.

As July sped to the door, Franklin whistled for Moose. The hound dove into the room, baying and blocking the woman's way.

Pointing at Mrs. Drunyon, Franklin ordered his hound, "Get her."

The Dragon stopped dead in her tracks as the dog pointed his tail and growled at her. With all her might, she flung the shoe at July. It hit the door post, vibrating the wall. The shoe bounced off the doorframe and thudded Moose in the back end. Moose yelped, twisted around, and barreled out the door after July. They ran until they hit the safety of July's house.

Dusty grass rose in a cloud about her and then settled as July skidded to a halt. Gramps was pounding a FOR SALE BY OWNER sign in the yard.

With The Dragon behind her and the For Sale sign ahead of her, July was in despair. She ran to Gramps and reached for the hammer. "No! No! No! You can't sell our home! Gramps, please, you can't," July sobbed.

Gramps laid the hammer on the ground and took the little girl in his arms. "Whoa … whoa … there, Sweetie. Let's calm down. Gramps will take care of you. It will be all right."

Moose lay at their feet, his head on his paws, his ear with the eyeglass earring resting across his nose. The hound whined a lonely cry.

The Meeting

"**MEETING** after school, May," Gramps informed Grams.

"Oh? How come?" Grams rolled her wad of dough, placed it in a crock bowl, and covered it with a dish towel before she turned. "July? What are you doing home?"

Gramps answered, "It's a long story, May. July poured it out once, so I'll give you the gist of it. The kids at school are calling Mrs. Drunyon names, and those kids that the teacher caught calling names have to meet after school with parents or guardians. That's us, May."

"What names?" Grams looked at her husband.

Gramps turned to July. "Go on and tell her."

July dropped her head and mumbled, "The Dragon."

"July!" Grams wiped her hands down her apron.

"I know it's not right, but she acts so much like a dragon. She is all the time breathing fire, and her temper is horrible," July wailed.

"She is an adult, and she is your teacher. In this house we respect both," Grams stated.

From outside, Aunt Sybil stormed to the screen door and thundered, "Anyone home?" She didn't wait for an answer. She pushed the screen door open and walked in. Levi and Celie were in tow.

"Good. I'm glad I caught you. Has July told you about the meeting after school today? The meeting which we are all required to attend?"

Gramps answered calmly, "Yes, Sybil, we know about the meeting."

"Just for the record, I am not happy about it. Levi and Celie have never been suspended from school before, and I hesitate to say it, but … "

"Then don't say it, Sybil," Gramps interrupted.

But Sybil continued, "Until July came here, my children were never in trouble. And I saw the sign out front letting all of Plevna know that your house is for sale. I suppose you think to move away from the 'shadow of delinquency.'" Sybil curved her forefingers in the air to create quotation marks. "You'll have to move clear out of the county, Ezra."

Gramps chuckled. "Until we find a place, Sybil, we thought we might move in with you. That's what family is for, right?" Gramps teased. Sybil gasped at the thought. "And it may take a long time to find a new place. One never knows," Gramps shrugged as he continued. "We may be your house guest for a long, long time, Sybil."

"That would be fun." Celie clapped.

"Fun? You would have to share your room with July," Levi chimed in.

"And you would have to give up your room for Grams and Gramps. Maybe you could sleep in the barn with the other animals," Celie joked.

Levi glared.

"That is enough, both of you." Sybil snapped her fingers. Levi and Celie hushed, but the faces they made at each other continued when their mama wasn't looking.

"Ezra, May, do you feel you are really qualified to take care of July in the way she needs?" Sybil laid her hand on her chest in feigned sincerity. "I mean with you being older, and grandparents ... and with July's background of a ... a ... alley ... " Sybil stuttered.

"Trash?" July blurted out.

It didn't even phase Sybil. "Exactly. Thank you for calling a spade a spade."

Gramps held his hand up to stop Aunt Sybil. "That is enough. The kids called their teacher a name, and they got caught. That is what kids will do, no matter where they are raised." Gramps threw his hands in the air in exasperation. "When I was in sixth grade, I put horse apples in my teacher's chair, so name calling is nothing."

Levi's face lighted at the thought. "Did your teacher sit on them?"

A pause settled over the room as everyone waited for the answer. "Only once, but I wouldn't advise doing it. It was very unhealthy for my backside when my father found out about it," Gramps confessed.

Sybil glowered at Levi. "That is unspeakable. Levi, you will not put horse apples in Mrs. Drunyon's chair."

Levi sobered, but a hint of a smile tugged at his mouth. "Yes, ma'am."

Gramps began again. "Sybil, we all agree the kids should not be calling Mrs. Drunyon names, but there are always two sides to a story. In Proverbs it says, 'He that answereth a matter before he heareth it, it is folly and a shame unto him.' Have you even asked your children what happened?"

"Ezra, I don't need preaching." Sybil pressed her lips in a grim line.

"I am a preacher. Now answer the question," he instructed.

Sybil sighed. "No."

Gramps turned to his grandchildren. "Levi? Celie?"

Celie started, "We really didn't call Mrs. Drunyon 'The Dragon.' It was Prissy who called her that, and Mrs. Drunyon caught her, well, she thought it was her. But we had agreed to turn the other cheek with Prissy, so July stood up as brave as David must have been with Goliath and said she was the one who called her The Dragon. Then Franklin, who has a crush on July, ups and says he's the one that called her The Dragon." Celie stopped for a breath then continued, "I felt sorry for Franklin, so I told Mrs. Drunyon that I did it. And I guess Levi didn't want to be left out so he said, 'I called you The Dragon.'"

"She threw a shoe at July and almost hit her in the head," said Levi.

Quietly Grams asked, "She threw a shoe at July?"

"Yep, and she has big, heavy shoes. It bounced off the wall and hit Moose. He yelped and ran. He probably ain't stopped running yet," Levi said.

"July, is that true? Mrs. Drunyon threw a shoe at you?" Gramps asked.

"Yes, sir," July answered.

Gramps was mad. "That … that … " he stammered.

"Woman." Grams kindly filled in the blank for him.

"That 'woman' ought not to be teaching. I am not happy about the meeting, but I will be there, and I will have my say."

Grams placed her hand on Gramps's arm. "We will be there, Ezra, but you need to calm down."

"Oh, I'll calm down. I will go to the church and pray. How much time do we have before the meeting?" Gramps asked, trying to calm himself.

Grams looked at the old clock on the kitchen wall. "A little over an hour."

"Good. I'll need every bit of it." After letting out a heavy sigh, Gramps turned to his daughter-in-law. "Sybil, is Luther working at the train station?"

Sybil nodded. "Until 7:00 tonight."

"See if he can get someone to sit in for him. I think it would be good to have the kids' father at this meeting. The more parents we have, the better," Gramps told her.

Sybil didn't argue. "Then we had best get going."

Franklin was sitting on the porch of the school when the Calendar clan arrived. Moose was beneath him with his nose poking out the step slats and resting his head on the first step. His ears splayed out with his earring sparkling in the afternoon sun.

"Where're your parents?" Levi asked.

"Ma's in the middle of pickling, and Pa's cutting what corn we got in this drought. He said calling names wasn't something worth time out of the harvest field, and Ma said she couldn't go off and leave her pickles a-boiling right now," Franklin explained. "Pa told me he was glad I was suspended. With my help for the next three days, he can have the harvest finished afore I have to come back to school," Franklin added.

"You lucky dog." Levi shook his head.

Franklin laughed. "Farming life is full of hard work. For three days, I'm gonna be hot, dirty, and tired. If you wanna come help, it would be fine by me."

Before Levi could answer, Prissy and her mother came around the corner. Prissy's mother had her face in a frown, and she was pulling Prissy by the arm. She stopped short, and July thought she reminded her of the old hen at Grams and Gramps's which always fluffed her feathers to make herself bigger and scarier than she really was. Although July thought she was really scary when she had to gather the eggs.

"Uh huh." Prissy's mother stopped in front of Gramps. "It looks to be almost a family affair. I don't know how my daughter got caught up in this, but I am sure it wasn't her idea."

Gramps cleared his throat. "Did you ask Prissy about it, Mrs. Overton?"

"Priscilla is a child. She undoubtedly was pulled into the situation without her knowledge," Mrs. Overton insisted.

Everyone looked to Prissy. A flush of color blanketed her face as she stumbled over the words trying to explain. "I was in trouble with Mrs. Drunyon, and July and Franklin and Celie and Levi helped me. Mother, Mrs. Drunyon is terrifying."

"How did you get in trouble with your teacher?" Prissy's mother asked.

Levi answered for her. "Prissy's the one that called her The Dragon, only Prissy didn't know Mrs. Drunyon had come up behind her."

Franklin added, "Yeah, Prissy was fixing to face The Dragon all alone. That's enough to scare anyone."

Mrs. Overton looked down at Prissy. "And you didn't tell me?"

Prissy shrugged. "You didn't ask."

"Young lady, is that all that happened?" her mother asked.

"Mother, Mrs. Drunyon threw a shoe at July and almost hit her right in the head. If July hadn't run out of the school, I don't know what Mrs. Drunyon would have done to her," Prissy answered honestly.

"Yeah, it did hit Moose, here." Franklin pointed at his dog. "He shot outta the school faster than lightening can strike. Finally, he wandered home, and I found him hiding in the barn," Franklin said. "He's okay, though. He come back to school with me to protect me from The Dragon."

"Who?" Gramps admonished.

Franklin stumbled to his feet. "Sorry, sir. He come along to protect me from Mrs. Drunyon."

Gramps nodded his approval. "That's better, Franklin."

Moose growled and yanked his head from between the steps. The schoolhouse door behind Franklin swung open, and a man no one had ever seen before stepped out and closed the door behind him. Franklin drew back to the side of the porch.

"Is everyone here for the meeting?" the man asked.

Franklin answered, "Everyone that's gonna come. My Ma and Pa can't make it."

"Very well." He pulled off his top hat. "I am Lucas Sheridan, legal representative for Mrs. Maxworth Drunyon. There will be no meeting at this time. Mrs. Drunyon would rather wait and cover everything at the hearing scheduled for Monday afternoon concerning property taken by a Miss July Calendar. Mrs. Drunyon feels this young woman was responsible for the actions of today, thus it can be addressed with the other charges. The rest of you need not be concerned."

July's heart pounded. *So a hearing has been set for Monday,* she mused.

Gramps's warm, strong hands rested on July's shoulders before he spoke. "Mr. Sheridan, we have a few questions we would like to ask Mrs. Drunyon, such as why she threw her shoe at my granddaughter?"

"Threw a shoe at your granddaughter? If I were you, I would check your information before I made extreme charges. I am sure my client would not stoop to actions such as that," Mr. Sheridan stated as he started to turn toward the door.

Gramps held up his forefinger to stay him. "I guarantee there are plenty of witnesses to the incident."

"Relations?" Mr. Sheridan inquired.

"Not all of them," Gramps answered.

Mr. Sheridan continued to question Gramps. "Children?"

"Yes," Gramps reluctantly admitted.

"Then I think we need not worry. If you will excuse me." Mr. Sheridan opened the door and closed it behind him.

In the quiet that fell over those left standing outside, they could hear Mr. Sheridan sharply questioning his client. "Mrs. Drunyon, did you throw a shoe at a student? I assure you, if that is the case, my fee will be double what I quoted you."

"When I have that ring, Mr. Sheridan, I intend to sell my house and leave this forsaken town. So whether I threw a shoe or not, I will have more than enough money to pay your astronomical fee," Mrs. Drunyon raged.

Something hit the floor with a thud. July hoped it was Mrs. Drunyon. If only she had died in the shed last summer, things would be so much easier, July imagined. She immediately had to bow her head and ask the Lord to forgive her for her thoughts.

17

The Hearing

THE courthouse in Plevna was not very big, and as with most small towns, it stood in the middle of the town square. As July looked to the top at the pigeon's roost, Gramps explained that even though there were three floors to the building, the third floor stood empty. The windows of the third floor reminded her of the attic windows at Grams and Gramps's. Both sets seemed to be eyes watching everything going on about them. She couldn't help remembering the first time she came to their house, and while staring at the attic windows, she thought she saw something move, even though the house was empty. Of course, it turned out to be Levi hiding upstairs, waiting to scare her. This made July wonder, though, if the third floor of the courthouse was really empty. The little girl shivered and thought of the saying, "A ghost just walked over your grave." She wondered how that could be possible since she didn't have a grave.

July spied Mr. Bryan coming their way. "Can I go meet him?" she asked. She had something to say to Mr. Bryan.

Gramps nodded, and July ran to talk to the man. "Did you get Mama's ring sold?"

"July," Mr. Bryan said. "I told you I wouldn't do anything illegal. I couldn't even try to sell it before this hearing. If the ring were found to belong to Mrs. Drunyon, we would be responsible for the value of it. Plus, I could get disbarred."

"But I got to be adopted to Grams and Gramps. There's no other way. They already put their house up for sale." July was desperate.

Mr. Bryan knelt on one knee and put his hands on her shoulders. "July, you are going to have to trust me on this one. I promise. I know what I am doing."

July felt squeamish inside. Mr. Bryan had been good to her from the time they had jumped off the train together and rolled to safety. He had believed her no matter what other people had said. "Okay, I'll try."

Mr. Bryan smiled. "That's all I ask." He looked around at all the people making their way to the courthouse. "I had hoped this would be a small gathering," he said. "Let's get Grams and Gramps and go in the back way. Then we won't have to talk to anyone."

That sounded like a good idea to July, and in no time, they were walking the back halls of the courthouse, their shoes clicking on the floors. It seemed every door they passed had a little peep window just high enough that July couldn't see how it did a bit of good. The hallway was cool, and she felt a bit of a breeze slither over her. "Did someone die in here? Is this place haunted?" she asked.

Mr. Bryan laughed. "I have thought so myself a time or two. It is said a couple of prisoners were killed when the jail was housed in the basement of this building. I'm not sure of the year, but I think it was back in the early 1890's. They were trying to tunnel out when one, Smack Thacker, I believe, found an old gold piece. With more digging, they stumbled on a rotten box full of those gold coins. Smack Thacker didn't want to share the find with his prison mate, Seldom Baker, so he made a noose of the shirt he wore and strung up his cellmate from the rafters. As Thacker was crawling through the tunnel, it collapsed and smothered him. It was three days before he was dug up."

"How much gold was there?" July asked.

"Now that is a mystery. There was only one gold piece found in Thacker's trouser pocket. Baker's coat pocket was empty except for a diary he had kept, telling of the gold. The gold was never recovered, and the story was just a nine-days' wonder. In other words, after nine days, the story was already old news."

July shivered. "Is the jail still in the basement?"

"No," Mr. Bryan told her. "That basement has been sealed off for years."

"Can you show me the basement real fast?" July asked enthusiastically, dreaming about what it would be like to find the gold.

"No. I doubt it would be safe, and we have more important business at hand. This is our door." He pulled it open for them and stepped to the side. "We'll wait here until it is time for the hearing. You can watch through this window, July. It's a one-way window, which means you can see them, but they can't see you."

July wasn't sure she wanted to see who all had come, but Gramps did. He reported over his shoulder whom he saw and who walked through the doors.

Mr. Bryan looked at his pocket watch then clicked it closed. "It's time. Are you ready, July?"

July shrugged. "I guess I'm as ready as I'll ever be." She took a deep breath and slid one of her hands in Gramps's rough hand and one in Grams's soft hand. Together they walked into the courtroom as muffled voices hushed.

On the back row, July was glad to see the faces of Franklin, Levi, and Celie sitting with Aunt Sybil and Uncle Luther. Franklin was alone, so July guessed his father was still harvesting corn. July stifled a giggle as she watched Moose shove his head, ears flopping, from behind Franklin's chair. She loved Moose's dangling earring. Across from them sat Prissy, her mother and a gentleman who must be Prissy's father. July glanced across the aisle to the table where The Dragon and her lawyer, Mr. Sheridan, sat. Just before she took her seat, she noticed Mr. Bryan's Aunt Tessie, who subtly nodded her head and winked. It gave July a warm feeling of encouragement.

An official man with a name plate saying "Bailiff" announced, "All rise." The judge walked in with robes flowing. The bailiff declared, "You all may be seated. This court will now come to order. The honorable Judge Benjamin Dooley presiding."

Judge Dooley pounded his gavel, and the session began. "We are here today to settle a civil matter between Mrs. Helen Drunyon and Miss July Calendar. I believe there is a question as to the ownership of a ring. Mr. Bryan, I understand you have that ring in your possession?" Judge Dooley asked.

Mr. Bryan stood and held out the ring that had belonged to July's mama. "Yes, Your Honor, I have the ring in question."

"Good." The judge turned to the bailiff. "Henry, bring me the ring."

The bailiff took the ring from Mr. Bryan and handed it to Judge Dooley. The judge studied the ring a minute before he asked, "Mr. Sheridan, would you have your client take the stand?"

"Yes, Your Honor." Mr. Sheridan turned to Mrs. Drunyon.

July watched as The Dragon walked to the bailiff who was ready with a Bible in his hand. As July heard the woman swear "to tell the truth," she wondered if that meant anything to The Dragon.

As Mrs. Drunyon sat, her lawyer began asking her questions. "Helen, tell us about the ring," he guided his client.

"That ring is my wedding ring. Maxworth placed it on my finger the day we were wed. I didn't take it off for years, but right before Maxworth passed, he asked for my ring. I don't know why he wanted it, but he was my husband, so I gave it to him. He passed away before he had a chance to give it back to me or tell me why he needed it."

"Helen, would you please describe the ring your husband gave you," her lawyer continued.

"Happy to oblige," Mrs. Drunyon began. "It's a simple ring. It's yellow gold with a diamond in it. I don't believe it cost much as times were tough when we married, but it meant much to us. I found a receipt when I was going through papers after Maxworth had passed. I believe it was for this ring with the price of $59.00. There was an extra charge of $2.00 for engraving. Maxworth had my initials, H. D. engraved inside the band. That is why I believe the receipt was for my wedding ring."

Judge Dooley held the ring to the light coming in from the outside windows. "Hmm. I see the D., but I cannot make out the H. It seems to have been sanded down or something of the like. There is some kind of scratch ... hmm ... maybe a J ... hmm. One would need a jeweler's glass to be sure."

Mr. Sheridan asked, "When was the ring last in your possession?"

The Dragon turned her head to stare at July. "It must have been in my things at the orphanage, and this ... this ... " She waved towards July. "This alley trash must have snuck into my room and rummaged through my things. She took it—stole it—that's what she did."

Mr. Bryan was on his feet. "Objection, Your Honor. Use of prejudicial language by the witness."

At the same time, Franklin jumped to his feet and blurted out from the back of the courtroom, "Alley trash? The Dragon called July alley trash? And we get in double trouble for calling her names, but she can do it? That's not fair."

"Sustained," replied Judge Dooley. He glared to the back row, and Franklin sat back down. The judge then turned toward the witness stand. "Mr. Sheridan, please inform your client that even though we are a small court, we do not allow name calling."

"Yes, Your Honor. We are sorry, sir. It won't happen again, will it, Mrs. Drunyon?" he warned.

The Dragon glared, but she conceded. "No."

Mr. Sheridan pulled at his ear. "Mrs. Drunyon, why do you think July Calendar took your ring?"

Mrs. Drunyon narrowed her eyes to glare at July. "Because she is the one who has it."

There was a ripple of laughter through the audience. Judge Dooley merely looked at the people, and a hush settled.

"Mrs. Drunyon, when did you discover the ring was in her possession?" Mr. Sheridan asked.

"On the train. I was escorting her to the custody of her grandparents when that ... " Mrs. Drunyon paused. "That child pulled it from beneath her blouse. It was strung on an old, dirty shoelace."

"Thank you, Mrs. Drunyon." Her lawyer turned to the judge. "That is all I have right now."

Judge Dooley thanked him and turned to July's lawyer. "Mr. Bryan?"

Mr. Bryan stood. "Mrs. Drunyon, between the time your husband, Maxworth, asked for your ring and the time you saw the ring hanging about July's neck, did you ever wear it?"

The Dragon blinked. "No."

"And why not?" Mr. Bryan continued.

"Because I didn't know where it was." Mrs. Drunyon spit out the words.

"Then how do you know you had the ring? How did the ring get in your things?" Mr. Bryan continued to hammer the witness. "You apparently didn't place the ring in your belongings because you didn't know you had the ring. You testified that your husband died before he was able to give it back to you."

"I figure Maxworth hid it in my things because he would have wanted me to find it sooner or later." Mrs. Drunyon was fuming and fast becoming a hostile witness.

"Mrs. Drunyon, I was also on that train when you chaperoned July Calendar into Plevna. Is it true that you physically tried to take the ring from this helpless ten-year-old girl?" Mr. Bryan asked accusingly.

"Helpless? Helpless my foot. I'll have you know she kicked me in the leg and jumped off the train. Does that sound helpless to you?" Mrs. Drunyon was seething.

"Mrs. Drunyon, before she jumped from the train, she was trying to escape from you. Is it true you snatched a gentleman's cane, raised it in the air, and tried to hit her with it? Isn't that why she ran and jumped from the train?" The lawyer leaned his head in close to hers.

"She stole my ring!" The Dragon shouted.

"And was this incident, chasing a child with a cane and threatening bodily harm, the reason you were fired from the orphanage you worked for?" Mr. Bryan calmly continued.

"Objection. Argumentative." Mr. Sheridan stood.

"I withdraw the question," Mr. Bryan stated.

A hush settled over the room. Mr. Bryan studied Helen Drunyon before he spoke. "At this moment, Your Honor, that is all the questions I have for this witness. However, I would like to retain my right to reexamine the witness at a later point."

"Very well." Judge Dooley dismissed The Dragon.

The whole court heard The Dragon's lawyer hiss in her ear, "I was not aware you chased a ten-year-old girl with a cane. Mrs. Drunyon how do you expect to win this case?"

"You are the lawyer. You have to win it," she demanded.

Judge Dooley sat back in his chair. "How about it, Mr. Bryan. Let's hear from your client."

Mr. Bryan nodded and escorted July to Henry, the bailiff.

Henry held the Bible low as he told her to place her right hand on the black book. "Do you swear to tell the truth so help you God?"

July swallowed. "Yes, I do."

Mr. Bryan led her to the stand and began to question her. "July, how did you get your mama's ring?"

"Objection, Your Honor," Mr. Sheridan interrupted. "It has not been established that it is her mother's ring."

Without waiting for the judge to reply, Mr. Bryan reworded the question. "July, how did you get the ring in question?"

"My mama gave it to me." July looked directly at Mr. Sheridan as she answered, "And it was my mama's ring."

Mr. Bryan put up his hand to stop July. "Just answer my questions, July, so we can prove ownership of the ring."

"Yes, sir." July responded obediently.

"And why did she give it to you?" Mr. Bryan gave July a knowing look.

"My mama and I lived in the alleys of Kansas City toward the end. I guess you could say we were both alley trash, like Mrs. Drunyon and Aunt Sybil call me." Silence settled in the courtroom, yet the tension was thick. Aunt Sybil sunk down in her chair.

July continued, "Mama was sick and couldn't hold a job, so we didn't have any money. Brutus stole mama's pocketbook. I don't know if his name was really Brutus. Everyone called him that because he was a big ol' brute, and he got by with whatever he wanted to do. Anyway, with her pocketbook gone, we didn't have any official papers either."

"How did you live, July?" her lawyer asked.

July blinked. She knew what the people would think of her.

"Go on, July," her lawyer coaxed.

July looked over the heads of everyone in the courtroom as her thoughts carried her into the past. "Mostly I would dig through dumpsters behind restaurants to find things to eat."

A breeze of horror swept over the courtroom gathering. Silent tears washed down Grams's face while Gramps slid closer and held her shaking shoulders.

Mr. Bryan continued, "July, winters are cold and hard in Kansas City. How did you stay warm?"

"Sometimes cardboard. Sometimes an old, empty building that had a broken window where we could get inside. I stole a blanket once to wrap Mama in because it was so cold." July's hands twisted nervously.

"July, why didn't you go to the authorities?" Mr. Bryan asked.

July pulled her thoughts back into the courtroom. "The police? Not on your life. They wanted to take me and stick me somewhere away from Mama. My mama was sick, and she needed me. I couldn't let them separate us. I was all she had, and she was all I had. We ditched the police every time we could. All of us alley people did."

Grams wasn't the only one crying now. Handkerchiefs, like white flags, flew all over the courtroom.

After a pause, Mr. Bryan asked, "July, when did your mother give you her ring?"

July closed her eyes then took a deep breath before she opened them again. "That last day. Mama wouldn't eat the crackers I found. She told me to save them for myself. I didn't know for sure, but I was afraid she was dying. That's when she gave me her ring." Silent tears were rolling unheeded down July's cheeks.

Her friend, Mr. Sam Bryan, handed her his handkerchief. "Go on, July."

July took the white cloth and twisted it. "Mama told me her ring was all she had. She wanted me to keep it to remember her by. She said it wasn't worth much except for memories." July sniffed before she went on. "Mama told me it was a key, but I didn't understand what she meant. I tried to ask her, but she started into one of her coughing fits. By the time it was over, I forgot all about it being a key. I never got another chance to find out what she meant." July's voice had dwindled to a whisper. "Mama's ring wouldn't fit my finger, so Mama told me to take my shoestring out of my shoe, and I did. I put the ring on the string and then tied it in a double knot around my neck so I wouldn't lose it. Mama smiled at the double knot and told me, 'I'm proud for you to have my ring, July.' Then mama just closed her eyes and died. That was the last thing she ever said to me."

Ladies were sniffing into handkerchiefs and dabbing at eyes. Celie was crying, and Levi swiped his arm across his nose. Franklin took his hands and swept the tears aside. Prissy's mother had thrown her hand over her gaping mouth while Prissy sat aghast. Even Mrs. Drunyon's lawyer had a handkerchief wadded to his nose as he leaned his head in his hand.

Mr. Bryan scanned the spectators in the courtroom before he asked, "July, did you have the ring when you went to the orphanage?"

"Yes, sir. I even wore it when I took a bath."

Levi and Franklin giggled. Aunt Sybil snapped her fingers to settled them down. Both slid down in their chairs and hushed.

"July, tell me about the events on the train," Mr. Bryan urged.

July turned her blue eyes to him as she answered. "First of all, if I had known Mrs. Drunyon thought my mama's ring was hers, I wouldn't have pulled it out in front of her. If I had taken the ring from her, I sure would have kept it hidden. I was just remembering my mama, and I like how the sun makes mama's ring sparkle. But when she saw it, she tried to yank it from me. She tried to get the conductor to hold me while she took it. Then she chased me with that man's cane. I had to get off that train before she hit me with it." The courtroom crowd moaned in sympathy.

"July." Mr. Bryan put his hand on top of hers. "This next question is a bit touchy, but I don't want you to be afraid to answer it."

July nodded.

"At the orphanage, what did the children call Mrs. Drunyon?" he asked pointedly.

July's hands flew to the sides of her face. "Mr. Bryan, do you want me to say that out loud?"

Mr. Bryan was very serious. "Yes, I do."

July dropped her hands. "The Dragon. They called her The Dragon." July was rigid with fear. She would be in trouble with Grams and Gramps for sure, and The Dragon was so close to her.

Again, giggles rose from the back where Levi, Celie, and Franklin sat. Gasps and a few chuckles twittered over the crowd. Mrs. Drunyon jumped to her feet, crashing her wooden chair against the half wall behind her. "I object." Then she glared at her lawyer. "Why are you not objecting?" She shoved her finger to his nose. "I'll have your hide for this, and you can forget the extra pay."

Moose heard The Dragon's roar and bolted. He scrambled from behind Franklin's chair and under Aunt Sybil's. The hound then shot from beneath Aunt Sybil's chair into the aisle. Aunt Sybil screamed and hopped atop her chair, holding her purse in one hand and her hat in the other. At the court's double doors, Moose howled and pawed madly on the floor, trying desperately to get out.

Prissy's mother was fanning herself, and Prissy's father was trying to keep her from sliding to the floor. "Mildred, get ahold of yourself. We are in public."

Mrs. Drunyon's lawyer stood, gathered his papers, and announced loudly, "You threw a shoe at a ten-year-old girl, and you chased her with a cane. You need to be locked up, and I will not help you take her dead mother's ring. No wonder they call you 'The Dragon.' It fits. I will send a bill for my fee." Mr. Sheridan shoved his papers into his briefcase, stuffed his handkerchief into his pocket, picked up his hat, and left the courtroom.

Moose skidded through the open door, tripping Mr. Sheridan, who landed on the slick floor. When he stopped sliding, he lunged to his feet, and everyone heard him say, "Come on Ol' Boy. I'll follow you out of this place." The lawyer and the dog's footsteps echoed down the hall.

The Revelation

AFTER Mr. Sheridan left, the judge let July go back and sit with her grandparents, but not before commotion had broken out in the courtroom.

In disbelief, someone exclaimed, "She threw a shoe?"

"And chased her with a cane?"

"A shoe?" someone said.

Another echoed, "She threw a shoe at that little girl?"

"She must be crazy."

"And she chased her with a cane." A man in the back raised his cane and waved it in the air.

"Chase her with that cane, and see how she feels," someone urged.

Judge Dooley smacked his gavel on his desk. "Order. Order in the court."

As all were calming, Judge Dooley leaned forward and tapped his finger on his desk. "Mrs. Drunyon, do you wish to proceed without counsel?"

"I want my ring, Judge," she spat.

"Very well." The judge leaned back in his chair as he addressed the court. "I am in a quandary. Legally, I believe the ring does belong to Mrs. Helen Drunyon, but my gut tells me the ring also belongs to this little girl. This gut also warns me that I could get lynched over this decision. I will need some time to deliberate." As he raised his gavel in the air, observers in the courtroom began shouting their own verdicts.

"Give it to the girl."

"The girl."

"You cannot take that ring from the little girl."

"Not her dead mother's ring. It would be wrong."

"God would never forgive us."

The Dragon whirled around as if she were ready to attack the people in the courtroom. Her hat slid over her forehead, its orange flower bobbing in front of her face, but she didn't seem to notice. Her fists were slammed into the sides of her hips. "It is my ring," she yelled as she stomped her foot.

Judge Dooley pounded his gavel. "Order in the court. There will be no more outbursts." He pointed his gavel toward the spectators. "If there are, I will adjourn to my chambers with only the litigants and Mr. Bryan, and settle this matter there."

People calmed themselves, and Mrs. Drunyon turned back to the judge. She wiped her hands on her skirts, stepped to her chair and sat, squirming to find a comfortable position. She patted her hair and straightened her hat.

Mr. Bryan approached the bench. "Judge, before you make a ruling, I do have one more witness."

Judge Dooley thumped the desk. "Then call your witness, Sam, and I hope it will shed some light on this case. I need some light."

Mr. Bryan nodded and announced, "I call Mrs. Tessie Henry."

The Dragon swung her head about. "Tessie?" The Dragon's eyes held fire as she jumped to her feet. "You're here? I thought you were out of the country."

Tessie smiled. "I was, Helen, until just a few days ago. That was when I found out you were back in little ol' Plevna, Kansas. You always said you would never come back here. I guess you changed your mind."

"Business. As soon as I finish this business, I am leaving this place, I assure you. I hope to never come back," The Dragon retorted.

Judge Dooley cleared his throat. "Ladies? Shall we continue?"

Tessie nodded, crossed to the bailiff and smiled warmly. "Henry, it's good to see you again."

Henry smiled at the informal greeting. "And you, too, ma'am. Just place your hand on the Bible and say after me, 'I solemnly swear to tell the truth, the whole truth and nothing but the truth.'"

Tessie repeated the words and took the stand with ease. Mr. Bryan grinned at the lady. Today she looked elegant in a deep purple hat with a matching suit. As always, she had a presence which commanded notice. A cluster of diamonds clamped on each ear were gathering light to throw dancing stars about the courtroom.

Sam asked his first question. "Tessie, do you have information which would 'shed light,' as Judge Dooley has requested, on this dual ownership of the ring?"

"Sam, I believe I do. I hate it has come to this, and I detest airing dirty laundry in front of so many of the good people of Plevna, but I know not how else to do it." Tessie looked to The Dragon.

Mrs. Drunyon demanded, "What are you doing, Tessie?"

"I am trying to thaw out your heart," Tessie explained. "We're sisters, Helen. You didn't used to be so hard. You cared about things. What happened to you?"

"Sisters?" July gasped. *How could they be sisters? They were nothing alike,* she thought.

Gramps held his finger to his lips to motion for July to stay quiet.

The Dragon shrugged. "Maxworth took money from the bank and left me to face this town alone. For the life of me, I don't know what he did with the money. It hasn't shown up anywhere. If I could have found it, maybe I could have given it back, so … so … these people would not hate me so much. You know, Tessie, how it was. No one would give me a job. They wouldn't talk to me. People looked at me with pity. Me, Helen Drunyon, the banker's wife!" she cried.

"Ahh, Helen. Remember what our parents taught us? When things go wrong, that's when you hold your head high and walk with courage. You are not what people decide. You are what you and the good Lord decide," Tessie spoke gently.

"I don't think the good Lord wants me either, Tessie," Mrs. Drunyon wailed.

"Helen, the good Lord does not condemn you for what your husband did, but God will find you guilty for what you stoop to." Tessie paused before she continued, "Now look at you. They call you The Dragon, Helen. The Dragon! And I see why. You are taking a precious ring from a child."

"But, Tessie, it's my ring. I have a right to my ring, and it's all I have left of Maxworth," The Dragon argued. "Besides, that girl is a thief; how else could she have gotten my ring?"

"Helen, first of all, you have a lot by which to remember Maxworth. He left you his house and his auto, and many precious memories," Tessie began.

"Not things like that, Tessie. Anyway, it doesn't matter one inkling. That ring is mine." The Dragon slapped her hand on the table in front of her.

"Helen, think about it," Tessie pleaded. "You're a teacher. Put two and two together. Do you remember your son, Maxworth Jr., and his infatuation with the Calendar girl?"

A gasp spread over the people of the court. Grams placed her hand over her heart. The judge allowed the sisters to continue to talk.

Tessie continued, "Helen, Max came to me."

"Why would he come to you?" Mrs. Drunyon asked. "He was my son."

"Helen, you would not listen to your son. Max assured me he had tried to talk to you, and more than once." Tessie tried to reason with her sister.

Mrs. Drunyon shook her head. "My Max, my son. I thought he would get over it. It was a mere crush."

Tessie went on, "He didn't get over it, and it wasn't a mere crush. It was real. Helen, Max loved that girl, and he wanted to marry her. You flat refused to even listen to him because you wanted someone of more 'social value' than the Calendar girl. Helen, you should have tried to get to know her. June was a sweetheart, and she loved your son. That's why they ran away together, but Max did talk to his father first."

Stunned, Mrs. Drunyon asked, "Max talked to Maxworth? And Maxworth agreed to them running away together?"

Tessie nodded. "Yes. Helen, your own husband gave Max your ring to use to marry June. He told Max he would get another for you. And it was your husband who told them to elope."

Mrs. Drunyon was shaking her head. "Elope?"

Tessie went on, "Before they could run away, the bank discovered that Maxworth had been embezzling money. Poor Maxworth decided to take the coward's way out and hanged himself."

"My poor Maxworth," Mrs. Drunyon droned.

Tessie smiled. "Helen, if you will think about it, there is a bright spot in all of this."

Mrs. Drunyon raised her head and looked doubtfully at her sister.

"Think about it, Helen. Now, I have no real proof, but I assume that July Calendar is your granddaughter," Tessie offered.

Most of the courtroom crowd gasped and watched in a trance. Grams pulled July close to her. Gramps put his arms about them both.

The Dragon slowly looked at July. "My granddaughter? Max's child?"

Chills ran up July's back, and she wanted to run. She wished she had never heard of Plevna, Kansas. *Was it possible? The Dragon was her grandmother?* she thought in horror.

The fire was slowly dying from The Dragon's eyes. "But … she … she looks nothing like my boy, Max."

"No? Looks aren't everything, Helen. She sure has spunk like he did. He had spunk enough to take what he wanted and run. This girl has had spunk enough to fight for what she believes is hers." Tessie smiled at the little girl.

The Dragon took a couple of steps closer to really see July for the first time. She held out her hands to the girl, but July shrunk away from her clutches. The Dragon threw her hands over her face and wailed, "Max's daughter? My granddaughter?" Then The Dragon began sobbing and collapsed to the floor.

July's world was whirling. Always she had wanted to know who her father was, but she never expected this. Her stomach turned. *The Dragon was her grandmother? Why did God let this happen? No one liked The Dragon. Think what Levi and Celie and Franklin would say.*

Gramps knelt in front of his granddaughter. "July, I want you to think hard about this. What would the Lord have you do? Can you turn the other cheek? Can you forgive Mrs. Drunyon?"

"I don't know, Gramps. I'm scared of her. She feels like The Dragon," July whispered.

"Let's say a little prayer?" Gramps offered.

July swallowed.

"Try?" he pleaded.

July stared at the woman on the floor before her. She drifted her gaze over the courtroom. People were frozen, watching what would happen. July whispered, "Please, Lord, help me to like The Dragon and be nice to her." A calm slipped over July.

"Can you do it, July? I know you are only ten, but God made you strong. With His help, you can do anything. Would you like to try?" Gramps asked.

The little girl nodded. "I think so."

Gramps gave her a little shove toward the woman piled on the floor. July tip-toed to her side and whispered, "Mrs. Drunyon?"

The lonely woman raised her head and looked at the child through mere slits in her swollen eyes. "I wish I were dead," was all Mrs. Drunyon could say.

"No, don't ever wish that." July had seen her mama die; she didn't want to watch that ever again, not even if it were The Dragon. The little girl knelt beside her.

"I have nothing to make me want to live. My Maxworth is dead, and for all I know, my son may be dead, too," she mumbled. "I may never know." The words haunted the courtroom. "No, I have nothing to live for."

"You have me, Mrs. Drunyon. I think I might be your granddaughter. Maybe you could get used to the idea, even if I am just alley trash." Slowly, July rested her hand on Mrs. Drunyon's shoulder.

Mrs. Drunyon gave a mournful cry. "I am so sorry, July. You are not alley trash—far, far from it."

"I couldn't help being alley trash," July whispered.

The woman on the floor, her face streaked with tears, muttered, "But, child, could you possibly like me? What is alley trash compared to The Dragon? That is who I am ... The Dragon. Everyone detests me. Don't you hate me, too?"

July shrugged. "I don't hate you. I'm kind of scared of you, but I don't hate you."

"What possible use could I be to you?" Mrs. Drunyon whimpered.

"I guess you could tell me about my daddy. I don't know much about him, and I always wanted to know him. I didn't even know his name until today." July was hopeful.

"I could. I would be happy to. But ... could you forgive me?" Mrs. Drunyon pleaded as if she were begging for her life.

"I think I could," July whispered. "I think it might be a good trade."

"Would you? Forgive me?" the worn woman choked, her head almost limp with no hope, waiting for July's answer.

July stood and crossed to the judge. "Could I have the ring, please?"

Judge Dooley dabbed his handkerchief across his nose. "Allergies," he lied. "Take your mama's ring, child."

July grasped the ring to her heart, walked to the fallen 'Dragon' and eased her to her knees. She took Mrs. Drunyon's hand and gently slipped the ring on her finger, the fine gold chain dangling from the woman's palm. "With this ring, I forgive you."

The old woman sobbed. She gazed at the long-lost ring, pulled it from her finger, and handed it back to July. "No, July. You take your mama's ring. Your mama wanted you to have it. Your father would have wanted you to have it, and I want it to be yours."

July looked up to Grams and Gramps. They had each other, and they had Jesus. Mrs. Drunyon didn't have a single soul. July didn't want to give up Grams and Gramps, but she wanted to help Mrs. Drunyon.

Grams and Gramps walked over. "Mrs. Drunyon, we would love to have you over for Sunday dinner. The pickins' might be skimpy, but we could get to know each other." Gramps held out his hand to help Mrs. Drunyon from the floor. "Family should know each other."

"Thank you, Ezra. I would like that very much," Mrs. Drunyon said.

"Good." Grams smiled.

"Helen, come and we'll walk you home." Gramps took her arm to steady her, then Grams took his place and put her arm in Mrs.

Drunyon's arm. Gramps then motioned to his granddaughter and settled her hand in Mrs. Drunyon's other hand.

July mouthed a thank you to Gramps as she took hold of Mrs. Drunyon's hand.

Gramps chuckled. "July, how about we go home and take down that For Sale sign?"

July's eyes sparkled. "First thing, Gramps."

Judge Dooley slammed his gavel down. "This court is now adjourned. All of you go home." It felt like the people of the court should clap. Some did, and some laughed, but all would talk about the happenings of today.

Sam Bryan winked at Tessie. "I think you had better reconsider that law degree. You just won your first case."

July looked to the ceiling with a thank you and slipped the gold chain with her mama's ring about her neck to nestle in its own comfortable place.

July's newly discovered grandmother gives her a box of her father's boyhood keepsakes, but it also contains a mystery she has decided she must solve!

Gift of December

Book 3 of the Calendar Series

Now available!

A secret pain that only love can heal.

Maggie's Treasure

Book 1 of the
Gatlin Fields series
Now available!

Only coals of kindness can save Maggie now.

In the Shadow of the Enemy

Book 2 of the
Gatlin Fields series
Now available!

A dark mystery puts Maggie in peril.

When Secrets Come Home

Book 3 of the Gatlin Fields series
Now available!

A hasty decision could prove to be fatal.

After the Dust Settles

Book 4 of the Gatlin Fields series
Now available!

Dustin determines to avenge
his mother's death even if
his father is a coward.

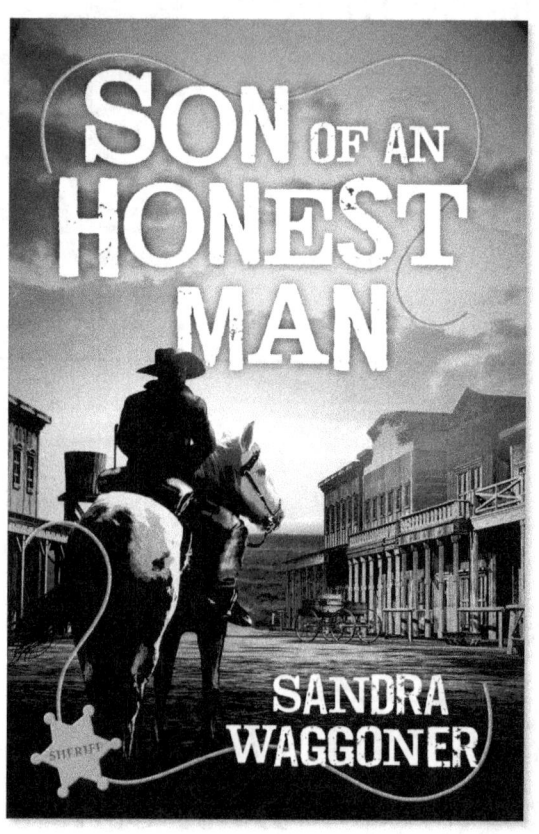

SON OF AN HONEST MAN

Now Available!

A DANGEROUS MISSION.
A DEADLY WOLF.
A DETERMINED YOUNG MAN.

DANGER AT WOLF ROCK

Now available!